INSIDE

MIIB™
MEN IN BLACK II

INSIDE

MⅡB
MEN IN BLACK Ⅱ

BRAD MUNSON

THE BALLANTINE PUBLISHING GROUP
NEW YORK

To Mary Jane, for everything

A Del Rey® Book
Published by The Ballantine Publishing Group
Copyright © 2002 Columbia Pictures Industries, Inc.

All rights reserved under International and Pan-American Copyright Conventions. Published in the United States by The Ballantine Publishing Group, a division of Random House, Inc., New York, and simultaneously in Canada by Random House of Canada Limited, Toronto.

Men in Black II TM & © Columbia Pictures Industries, Inc. All Rights Reserved.
All Mercedes-Benz elements are the intellectual property of DaimlerChrysler, © 2002. All Rights Reserved
Twister ® & © 2002 Hasbro, Inc. Used with permission.

Del Rey is a registered trademark and the Del Rey colophon is a trademark of Random House, Inc.

Photo credits: Melinda Sue Gordon, Phillip V. Caruso, Holly Haines, and Industrial Light & Magic

Interior book design: Michaelis/Carpelis Design Assoc. Inc.

www.delreydigital.com
www.MenInBlack.com

Library of Congress Catalog Card Number: 2002102315

ISBN: 0-345-45526-6 (Hardcover)
      0-345-45065-5 (Trade Paperback)

Manufactured in the United States of America

First Edition: June 2002

10 9 8 7 6 5 4 3 2 1

ACKNOWLEDGMENTS

Books like *Inside MIB II,* crammed with pictures, anecdotes, and "artifacts," always require the outstanding efforts of a great many people working far too many hours on incredibly tedious projects. At the risk of leaving someone out, I'd like to single out a few who went above and beyond the call, including Heidi Holicker at Cinovation, Stephen Keneally at Industrial Light and Magic, and, most especially, Cindy Irwin at Sony Pictures Consumer Products. And a very special thanks *has* to go to *MIB II* associate producer Stephanie Kemp, who always returned the phone calls and had all the really *good* stories. This would be a whole lot of very blank pages without their help.

CONTENTS

INSIDE

MIIB™

MEN IN BLACK II

CHAPTER 1

WE'RE
B-A-A-A-ACK

Don't look.

Wait. Okay, right there, out of the corner of your eye.

Does that mail carrier have a tail? A big ol' scaly one—*there*, see, he's tucking it away. Now it just looks like he's got a big butt.

And *there*. Why are there fireflies floating in a pattern, around that couple riding the bicycle built for two? Why is that dog over there *watching* you? And...and did that cockroach just *say something?*

It's possible—just *possible*, mind you—that there's a whole world around you—around *us*—that we don't even suspect is there. A world much larger than the comfortable, simple place we live in every day. A world of high adventure, low cunning, giant bugs, and Arquillian War Armadas.

The world of the Men in Black. The world of Agents Jay and Kay (and all the other letters), those beat cops of the impossible who protect humankind from the scum of the universe.

Moviegoers around the globe got their first glimpse of this amazing world around us—as well as under and over and inside us—in 1997's *Men in Black.*

And now, with *Men in Black II,* we're going back.

It's just like you remember it...only *better.*

Inside *Inside MIB II*

Just about everybody who made the original *Men in Black* movie work returned for *MIB II.* Producers Walter Parkes and Laurie MacDonald, who developed the original concept from Lowell Cunningham's Malibu comic book series, worked for months with screenwriter Robert Gordon to build the first draft of the new script. Director Barry Sonnenfeld returned, as well, bringing his unique sense of humor and timing to the project. Tommy Lee Jones is back as Agent Kay; Will Smith is back as Agent Jay. So is Rip Torn as Zed, and Tony Shalhoub as the grungier-than-ever Jeebs, he of the exploding head. Frank the Pug, the world's pushiest talking dog, is back in a big way, as are the Worm Guys and even the security guard who sits by the door.

There's a great new villain in Lara Flynn Boyle's Serleena, and an equally great new villainous sidekick (and a half) played by Johnny Knoxville of MTV's *Jackass.* There's even a love interest for Jay in Rosario Dawson of *Josie and the Pussycats*, and more Rick Baker aliens—new and returning—than you can stuff into a sack.

But what's most important is that the *world* of *Men in Black* is still the same strange, exciting world that's wrapped around our own, the one that's just around the corner, just beyond our perception. The world that's out there to explore, if we only know how to find it.

These Eyes-Only, Declassified Files provide a glimpse of that world—the parts that appear in the sequel, and the parts that never quite made it. We'll poke into the corners of the MIB, look at the unexpected heroes and brand-new villains. We'll talk with the producers and directors and stars, and you'll see things you won't see anywhere else—not even up on the screen. You'll encounter a huge collection of behind-the-scenes images, from on-the-set production stills to concepts drawings to makeup tests.

It's going to be a fast and funny ride through the unexpected, just like the movie itself. And it all starts *here...*

The Same Old Interstellar Love/Chase/Amnesia Story

You've seen the movie. You've read the script. Now enjoy the summary:

Four years have passed since Agent Kay (Tommy Lee Jones) was neuralyzed and retired as a Man in Black. Now his former partner, Agent Jay (Will Smith), is a legendary agent in his own right...and more burned out than Kay ever was. Cut off from all personal contact, he lives-eats-breathes MIB. He can't seem to keep a partner; his original recruit, Agent Elle, returned to the morgue from whence she came, and he has a bad habit of neuralyzing anybody else he's teamed with.

As the story opens, Jay saves New York from the rampage of a giant worm—Jeff the Worm—riding it bareback through the subway. He pauses just long enough to send yet another temporary partner—Agent Tee (Patrick Warburton)—into early retirement with his "little flashy memory thingy," and then returns to work.

What he doesn't know yet is that a menace from twenty-five years earlier—a techno-organic she-creature from the Kylothian Empire named Serleena—has come to Earth in search of her civilization's greatest treasure and power source: the Light of Zartha. Landing in Central Park, Serleena (Lara Flynn Boyle), takes on the form of a Victoria's Secret model she glimpses in New York Magazine, *dresses in the shape-shifted remains of a leather coat she steals from a mugger she eats in passing, and locates her terribly unsuccessful agent, Scrad/Charlie (Johnny Knoxville), a two-headed...mutant? ...with a taste for American pop culture and no class at all.*

Together they go to interrogate Ben, owner of Ben's Famous Pizzeria of Soho. Ben is a Zarthan in human drag who may or may not know where the Light is being hidden. Neither Serleena nor Scrad/Charlie notices Laura, Ben's longtime friend and employee, who cowers in the next room as the Kylothian villainess cuts Ben out of his human suit and lets him dissolve. Just before he dies, Ben confirms that the Light is on Earth...but that it will be leaving in less than twenty-four hours, to be returned to Zartha, and therefore lost to Serleena and the Kylothians forever. Serleena stalks out, a plan already forming in her diabolical mind, and Laura calls the cops.

It's not the cops who answer—it's the Men in Black. And soon it's Agent Jay himself, with his newest partner in tow—none other than Frank the Pug, fresh from the MIB mailroom. Jay is affected by the warmth and beauty of the young woman, and on an impulse he doesn't neuralyze her after she's answered all his questions...he takes her out for pie. With the information she supplies, and having located Serleena's ship in Central Park, Zed and the MIB piece together the truth: Serleena's back and she's still looking for the Light...the Light that was supposed to have left Earth twenty-five years earlier, through the actions of the now-departed Agent Kay.

Clearly, only Kay himself can solve this mystery...and his memory was wiped away long ago. So now it's Jay's job to pull Kay back into the world of the MIB, restore his memory, and find the Light of Zartha before Serleena does...and he needs to do all of this before the Light's fail-safe triggers the end of the world.

Jay and Frank visit Truro, Massachusetts, where Kay, now known as Kevin Brown, serves as postmaster. Jay confronts him directly, but of course Kay—who, other than remembering nothing about the MIB, seems remarkably unchanged—doesn't believe a word of it...at first. Then Jay reveals that virtually everyone who works in the Truro Post Office is an alien in disguise—that's why he likes it there, he's comfortable with them. And so the puzzled Kevin returns to MIB Headquarters in New York, where a beautiful, high-tech machine will be used to restore his memory. Then he can tell them what he really did with the Light of Zartha.

Back at headquarters, Jay sheds himself—so to speak—of his canine partner, and takes Kay in for deneuralyzing...just as Serleena and Scrad/Charlie show up at the Immigration Center, and the Kylothian proceeds to take over the entire MIB Headquarters with her devastating "neural roots," binding agents in techno-organic brambles, while releasing hundreds of hardened alien criminals. Jay and Kay, hidden in the Deneuralyzer Room, are "flushed"—literally washed out of the building in an emergency security action that seals the HQ from the outside world. Now they're on their own. They have to save MIB and find the elusive Light, all as soon as possible...and they still haven't restored Kay's memories.

They're forced to turn to their sleazy old informant "friend," Jeebs, who's still selling illegal offworld technology from his grubby little pawn shop, though he's also made a small fortune on the Internet. Turns out Jeebs has a homemade deneuralyzer in his basement—one he's been trying to get rid of for years—and after some "persuading," he agrees to use it on Kay.

But mere moments after the transverse energy surges through Kay—and nearly blows his brains apart—Jeebs's basement is invaded by alien thugs, sent by Serleena to capture the agents. Kay, still dazed, flees to the street. Jay stays to fight a losing battle, and only Kay's heroic last-minute return, memory seemingly restored, saves his life. They escape to continue the search for the Light.

Actually, Kay's memory isn't fully restored. He remembers everything about his past life with the MIB...except the bit about the Light of Zartha. Seems he neuralyzed himself *some years earlier, to keep that secret away from everybody. With MIB HQ still in the clutches of Serleena, Jay and Kay head back to the pizzeria, and Laura. There, Kay deciphers a series of arcane clues that lead him to a key—a key to a locker in Grand Central Station—while Jay, still very taken with Laura, chooses once again not to neuralyze her, but instead decides to take her to a safe place, where he believes Serleena can't reach her. They drop her off at the groovy bachelor pad owned by the infamous Worm Guys of the MIB.*

The agents leave her there playing a rousing game of Twister *with the worms, and head to Grand Central Station...where they find an amazing civilization hidden in Locker C-18 (the locker that fits Kay's key). The tiny inhabitants of Lockertown worship Kay as a god, and give him the cheap Timex and video rental card he left with them twenty-five years earlier. The watch seems to be some kind of timer, counting down to a Zero Hour that's now less than sixty minutes away.*

Serleena is enjoying her control of MIB Headquarters, using the released criminals in all sorts of creative endeavors—particularly a large cone-shaped alien genius named Jarra—and torturing Zed, just for the heck of it. Even Scrad and Charlie are having second thoughts about Serleena's mad scheme, but they're too chicken to do anything about it.

Meanwhile, Jay and Kay are on the move. The video card has led them to Tapeworm, a grubby little video store operated by Newton (a familiar face from Men in Black*), who in turn hands over a videotape that Kay had reserved decades earlier. It's an episode of the documentary series* Mysteries in History, *hosted by Peter Graves—an exceedingly low-budget production about the Men in Black and the Light of Zartha. It's cheesy, but it's enough to trigger Kay's full memory of the actual event. It's true: He didn't send the Light offplanet, as he had been ordered. He had gone offbook—he'd let his personal feelings get in the way, because he had loved the beautiful Zarthan Princess Lauranna.*

Now they know where the Light is—it's on Laura's bracelet! They rush back to the Worm Guys' pad, but Jay makes the mistake of calling Frank back at MIB HQ first, to tell him where they're headed. Serleena intercepts the call...and by the time they make it to the worms' place, the Bad Guys have already taken Laura and cut all the worms in half. Not that that's a bad *thing, necessarily...each piece regenerates, and it just means there are twice as many worms now. And they're mad. The agents make a quick visit to Kay's old apartment to gather weaponry; the worms arm themselves, as well, in the best Rambo style, and together the agents and the worms attack MIB Headquarters, blowing through the front doors and creeping through the air vents to wrest control back from Serleena and her henchmen.*

Jay encounters Jarra, who is guarding Laura, and fights a set of airborne, homicidal, miniature versions of Jarra. He beats them and rescues Laura. Meanwhile, Kay confronts Serleena and nearly dies, but a surprisingly militant Zed and Jay blow her away with a good ol'-fashioned shotgun.

Now it's a race to get the Light—apparently it's in Laura's possession—off the planet before the deadline. Otherwise its fail-safe will be activated, and it will destroy the planet.

But Serleena isn't finished. Even as Jay, Kay, and Laura fly through the streets of Manhattan in their highly modified Mercedes-Benz, zooming to the Light's point of departure, the revived Kylothian gives chase in an insectile spaceship that Jarra had cobbled together for her. The agents try to evade her, but they just can't throw her off...until Jay drives the super-Mercedes-Benz into the subway tunnels, where he leads Serleena right into the angry, gaping maw of Jeff the Worm, still ticked off from Jay's bareback ride at the beginning of the movie. She's eaten whole...and the agents make it to the New York rooftop overlooking the harbor and the Statue of Liberty, where a beam from a star above the Statue of Liberty transforms a piece of abstract sculpture into the ship that will carry the Light away from Earth, back to Zartha itself.

But Serleena still isn't done. She reappears yet again, transforming poor Jeff the Worm into a vast, powerful, and really ugly techno-organic monster that attacks Jay on the rooftop in a mass of flailing, deadly vine-tentacles. Jay struggles to escape, but fails....It's only the last-minute intervention of Scrad and Charlie—seeking political asylum and offering up a proton detonator—that destroys Serleena once and for all, and allows the Light of Zartha to leave the planet at the very last moment in a dazzling light show that can be seen all over New York City.

Not to worry, however. The MIB can still cover it up in grand style—they always do. The torch of the Statue of Liberty shines brightly over New York Harbor—with the light of a gigantic neuralyzer!

There it is. Just your typical love/chase/amnesia/end-of-the-world story line. You've seen it before...but this time, it's done with *style*.

"The Script Comes First"

It all began with Walter Parkes and Laurie MacDonald, the hugely successful producers of the original *Men in Black*, also the heads of production at DreamWorks SKG.

Actually, more accurately, it began *inside* the first movie.

"There were a number of different plots that came and went in [preparing] the first movie," Walter Parkes said, "and virtually every one of them ended with the neuralyzation of Tommy Lee Jones's character...which always left us with the possibility that—should there be a second film—we would have a ready-made story: The teacher becoming the student." The sequel, it seemed obvious, would feature a case the roots of which would be buried deep in Kay's memory, and somehow Jay would have to re-initiate him into the world of the Men in Black. "It wasn't, 'Oh, wouldn't it be great to create a franchise,'" Parkes revealed. "It was just intrinsic, even in the very first movie."

The relationship between Jay and Kay was a cornerstone of the original movie's success, so Tommy Lee Jones and Will Smith were "must-haves" for *MIB II* from the outset. But Parkes and MacDonald knew there was more to it than that. *MIB* was about a whole *world*—a look and feel that was unique, and quirky, and endless in its potential. "Movies nowadays are as much about the places they take you as the stories they tell you," Parkes said, "and there's something about the world of the Men in Black that audiences are interested in revisiting."

The producers and Sony Pictures Entertainment executives were interested in exploring that world further, but only if it could be done right, and it was after a year of struggling to put together a deal in the abstract that Parkes and MacDonald realized there was one thing they needed first and foremost to make this movie real: *a script*.

"It was very hard," Parkes recalled. "People were involved in these business discussions without a particular target or focus. I mean, it's very nice to say in the abstract, 'Let's make a sequel to *Men in Black*,' but it's all just chitchat until you have a hundred twenty pages you can read and say, 'Boy, that's fantastic, I want to do that.'"

"We've always worked that way on projects in general," Laurie MacDonald said. "Obviously the deals are very complicated, but it's very difficult to get things moving without a script." So the husband-and-wife producer team turned to Robert Gordon, with whom they had already enjoyed success on *Galaxy Quest*, another sci-fi movie with a remarkable amount of human warmth and character. Ultimately, they would spend a year working with him on that first version of the *Men in Black II* script, long before any of the stars or even the director were attached.

And it was the existence of that first-round script that made *MIB II* a reality. "Suddenly there was something on the table," MacDonald said. "And between that and people's desire to be part of the second movie, we were actually able to get everyone together to make this movie."

Associate Producer Marc Haimes recalled that working this way was a challenge for Gordon, as much as for Parkes and MacDonald. "Up to that point," Haimes said, "Bob had been a very solitary writer. With both *Galaxy Quest* and his earlier picture, *Addicted to Love*, he went off and he wrote, and then he turned it in." But this was a big sequel for a big franchise, and it was going to have to be more of a collaboration. Bob Gordon had never worked that way before, "but he loved it," Haimes said.

"Those meetings were so much fun, trying to figure out where to go," he added. "And it's amazing, if you go back and look at that original outline, how many of the ideas are still in the movie."

The Loneliness of the Long-Distance MIB Agent

There were really two major inspirations that drove *MIB II* forward. One was the final secret of the Light of Zartha—a plot point that was worked out very early on. And the other was the challenge of character that Will Smith's Agent Jay was facing: the hard, cold fact of the loneliness inherent to his chosen line of work, the isolation that was as much a part of being a Man in Black as were the excitement and the secrets.

"One of the things I really like about the movie," Barry Sonnenfeld noted, "is that not only are these guys heroes, not only do they save the world, but no one can ever thank them for it. They can't; they don't exist. And that's *lonely*."

It was a key point for everyone involved, from the producers to the writers and director to the stars themselves. It's even reflected in one of the early versions of the script for the *first* movie— when Jay is thinking of becoming a Man in Black, and he asks Kay, "What's the catch?"

"The catch," Kay tells him, "is that you will sever every human contact. No one will ever know you exist anywhere. Ever."

"Is it worth it?" the younger man asks.

"Oh, yeah," Kay says immediately. "It's worth it. If you're strong enough."

Now, four years later, Agent Jay's strength is beginning to wane. He's obsessed with work; he misses his old friend; he longs for exactly the kind of human contact being a Man in Black prevents. And once in a while—just *once* in a while—he'd like to get a little credit.

Jay's dilemma is most obvious in his talk with Agent Tee, just before Jay mercifully neuralyzes the big doofus. "You like being a hero," Jay says, and Tee admits it—yeah, he does. "Then you joined the wrong organization," he tells him. "You ever heard of James Edwards? He saved eighty-five people on the subway tonight, and nobody even knows he exists. And if no one knows he exists, no one can ever love him."

Agent Jay's original name was James Darrel Edwards III.

"It must be hard," Laura Vasquez says to Jay, somewhat later in *MIB II*. "Keeping secrets, never knowing anyone. Must be very lonely."

Jay doesn't disagree with her.

"That's the [cost] of being a Man in Black," Associate Producer Marc Haimes said, "and that's what we wanted to explore this time around."

It took the better part of a year, two full drafts, and countless revisions, but it was that first Robert Gordon script—with Serleena (in a somewhat different form), the Light of Zartha, Scrad/Charlie, Frank the Pug, the return of Kay's memory, his renewed partnership with Jay, and the exploration and ultimate understanding of the loneliness of the Man in Black—that went to Will Smith, Tommy Lee Jones, Barry Sonnenfeld, and many of the other key members of the creative team. After a fair amount of courageous support and backing from Sony Pictures Entertainment, those people started saying yes. The old team began to reassemble.

Coming Home

One of the things that has distinguished this sequel from countless others is just how *many* people, in front of the camera and behind it, were willing and able to return for a second round. "Everybody likes to be involved in a *successful* movie," Production Designer Bo Welch pointed out, and certainly *Men in Black* was a major success for Sony Pictures. "The experience of the first movie was a very happy one," Laurie MacDonald recalled. "I think everyone involved was interested in coming back."

A great deal of that eagerness had to do with the atmosphere that Barry Sonnenfeld created every day on the set. "It's very hard to create spontaneity in the context of a very difficult production," Parkes noted, "but Barry Sonnenfeld keeps things very, very loose."

"And *MIB II* is as technically complicated as a movie can be," MacDonald agreed. "But Barry manages to create this connection with his actors, and keeps the comic attitude of the movie going on between takes. I think people really enjoyed the experience."

They must have. Beyond Parkes and MacDonald themselves, there was quite a list of returnees:

BARRY SONNENFELD, DIRECTOR. By all accounts, as offbeat as he can appear, Barry Sonnenfeld is very smart, very loyal, and very *busy*. Before the first *Men in Black*, he was a highly successful cinematographer, working with just about everybody, beginning with *Blood Simple* and continuing through (among others) *Throw Momma from the Train*, *Big*, *When Harry Met Sally*, *Miller's Crossing*, and *Misery*. His first director's gig was *The Addams Family*—a hit large enough to generate a sequel, *Addams Family Values*, which he also directed. In 1995, Sonnenfeld produced and directed Elmore Leonard's *Get Shorty* with John Travolta, and shortly after *Men in Black*, produced *Out of Sight,* considered by most to be George Clooney's breakout film in his leap from *ER* to the big screen—not to mention a nice little showcase for Jennifer Lopez. After *MIB* came *Wild Wild West,* with Will Smith in front of the camera and many of the usual suspects behind the scenes, and *Big Trouble,* starring Tim Allen and featuring—remember this name—Johnny

Knoxville. Barry also produced *The Tick* (starring Patrick Warburton—aka Agent Tee) for Fox Television, and directed its pilot. In years past, he had served as producer for three other TV series as well: *Maximum Bob, Fantasy Island,* and *Secret Agent Man.*

Then, of course, there's Barry the Legend, the guy who is proud to demonstrate his personal self-defense techniques to Tommy Lee Jones: techniques like lying on his back and waving his arms and legs in the air. The guy wears a white cowboy hat and a pink cowboy shirt while riding around East Hampton on a Vespa. He's also a man who inspires tremendous loyalty among his coworkers and partners. Over the years, he's pulled together a team that travels with him from picture to picture, project to project...and shows no signs of breaking up.

GRAHAM PLACE, COPRODUCER. "He's worked with Barry forever," said Walter Parkes, "and they're a perfect match. He's like the Perry Como of the production. He never gets rattled, never gets ruffled. You never see him sweating it out, but things just get *done*. He and Barry work together in spite of being very different kinds of people." Blond, bearded, and quiet, Place is the backbone of the operation, the moneyman, the logician…and the perfect balance to Barry Sonnenfeld.

BO WELCH, PRODUCTION DESIGNER. One of the most distinctive and striking designers in Hollywood, Bo Welch has created more memorable images and extraordinary movie environments than just about anybody. The partial list includes: *The Lost Boys, Beetlejuice,* and *Ghostbusters II* in the 1980s, along with *Edward Scissorhands, Batman Returns, Wolf, A Little Princess,* and *The Birdcage* in the 1990s, all before *Men in Black.* After *MIB,* he worked with Barry again on *Wild Wild West* and *The Tick,* where he also directed two episodes, and he will be taking on the Caped Crusader again in a whole new context—as production designer on the upcoming *Batman: Year One.* Lanky and soft-spoken, Bo Welch's vision informs every page of the script and every scene in the film, from the set design to the gadgetry to the overall feel of the production. He, along with Rick Baker and Barry Sonnenfeld, formed a kind of "creative triumvirate" that conceived and maintained the world of the Men in Black.

RICK BAKER, CREATURE SPECIAL EFFECTS MAKEUP DESIGNER. Actually, Rick Baker's elaborate title as found in the credits doesn't begin to define his role on *MIB II.* Baker, along with Bo Welch and Barry Sonnenfeld, was a key conceptual thinker on the picture. A multiple Oscar winner for *How the Grinch Stole Christmas, Men in Black, The Nutty Professor, Ed Wood, Harry and the Hendersons,* and *An American Werewolf in London*—and nominated nearly half a dozen other times—Baker is a living legend among makeup people, beginning with his work on *King Kong* in

OPPOSITE
DIRECTOR
BARRY SONNENFELD.

ABOVE LEFT
COPRODUCER
GRAHAM PLACE WITH
SONNENFELD, WHO SAYS HE IS
"STILL MY BEST FRIEND IN THE
WHOLE WORLD."

ABOVE RIGHT
RICK BAKER TALKS
WITH BARRY SONNENFELD.
NOTE BAKER'S BLACK MIB SUIT
AND SONNENFELD'S COWBOY HAT
AND BOOTS. IT'S HOLLYWOOD;
EVERYONE HAS A COSTUME.

1976—when he actually put on the suit and *played* Kong—then *Star Wars* in 1977, straight through Tim Burton's 2001 remake of *Planet of the Apes*. The legend begins, of course, with his extraordinary creatures—the latex masks, the bodysuits, the prosthetics that he used to create virtually all the aliens in the picture. But Baker's influence goes far beyond that. It was his vision, matched to and informed by Bo Welch's production design, that dictated the look and feel of virtually *all* the nonhuman characters in *Men in Black II*, including the creatures ultimately produced by Industrial Light & Magic (ILM). He also had a profound effect on everything from set design to costuming. His creative inspiration is seen everywhere in this movie—and felt throughout the industry.

Other returnees include Costume Designer Mary Vogt, Prop-Master Doug Harlocker, Composer Danny Elfman, Script Supervisor Mary Bailey, Set Decorator Cheryl Carasik, and Associate Producer Stephanie Kemp. All welcomed the chance to reenter the world of the Men in Black.

And then there are the actors:

TOMMY LEE JONES (AGENT KAY). A rancher and a Harvard graduate, as well as an intelligent and articulate actor, Jones was one of the models for Oliver in Erich Segal's *Love Story* (along with his college roommate, Al Gore)—and went on to costar as Oliver's roommate in the film version. His polished, taciturn, and still-accessible characterizations are memorable in a wide range of genres, from *Coal Miner's Daughter* to *The Amazing Howard Hughes*, from *Lonesome Dove* to *The Fugitive*. And he takes chances, too, playing Clay Shaw in *JFK*, Dwight McClusky in *Natural Born Killers*, and Ty Cobb in *Cobb*. He seems fearless at times, ready for any challenge. Still, *Men in Black* was Tommy Lee Jones's first serious stab at comedy, and he credits Barry Sonnenfeld with convincing him that he really *could* be funny on film, if he had a mind to. Jones was the first person attached to the original *Men in Black*, according to Parkes and MacDonald—even before Barry Sonnenfeld. "We knew we had to have him," Parkes said. "Earth-bound, bluesy, a Fifties investigator that you actually *believe* could handle a gun. Will Smith, and the chemistry that happened between them, was a great gift, but we knew from the outset that Tommy Lee Jones was our anchor."

WILL SMITH (AGENT JAY). *Men in Black* was still in production when Will Smith's first huge hit exploded: *Independence Day*. Overnight, he went from an up-and-coming TV comedian to a *star*, and it hasn't stopped since. His first action picture, *Bad Boys*, is less than seven years old, and since then, Smith has become a major action star whose credits include both *MIB* pictures, *Wild Wild West*, and *Enemy of the State*. He is also a respected and increasingly accomplished "serious" actor, with projects beginning with *Six Degrees of Separation* in 1993 and continuing to his acclaimed performance in *Ali*. Exuberant, funny, very bright, and incredibly charming, Smith had as much to do with setting the tone on the set as Sonnenfeld, keeping everyone comfortable and laughing even during the most tedious technical challenges. *MIB II* benefited from his "buff-up" for *Ali*, as well; it's evident in his sleek new physique and in his performance of the increasingly strenuous stunt action.

RIP TORN (ZED). He's the voice of Zeus. He's every smarmy executive or bullying politico you've ever met. He's an accomplished man of theater, a consummate professional, and he's got well over a hundred movies and TV projects to his credit, including Disney's animated *Hercules*, *The Larry Sanders Show*, *The Man Who Fell to Earth*, and *The Insider*. He's seventy years old and he hasn't even begun to slow down. He even played Tommy Lee Jones's father—Big Daddy—in a production of *Cat on a Hot Tin Roof* years ago. "At our very first *Men in Black* read-through," Associate Producer Stephanie Kemp recalled, "we had Will, Johnny, and Rip—about half the cast in all. Rip comes in from Connecticut; he sits down, and maybe he's read the script and maybe he hasn't. But every line out of his mouth is hilarious. He's not even *doing* anything, but he's *got* it, and he's *perfect*—that's the beauty of Rip."

TONY SHALHOUB (JEEBS). Since his rise to national prominence as Antonio, the Italian cabdriver on NBC's television series *Wings*, Tony Shalhoub has built an impressive career as a character actor in drama and comedy. From his affecting performance as Primo in *Big Night* to his harrowing portrayal of Frank Hadid in *The Siege*, Shalhoub has proven himself to be a thoughtful and skilled actor. Prominent directors have seen that, as well, including the Coen brothers for *The Man Who Wasn't There*, Robert Rodriguez for *Spy Kids*, and Mike Nichols for *Primary Colors*. On the set, Shalhoub's gift for improvisation was enviable, his professionalism and preparation impressive. And there was nothing quite like seeing Will Smith cutting up, and tech people running in all directions...and Tony Shalhoub, in full Jeebs makeup, sitting tranquilly in his Barcalounger, reading *The New York Times*.

BELOW LEFT
TOMMY LEE JONES (AGENT KAY), THE FIRST STAR ATTACHED TO THE FIRST PICTURE, AND ONE OF THE "MUST-HAVES" FOR THE SEQUEL. "WE KNEW FROM THE OUTSET THAT TOMMY LEE JONES WAS OUR ANCHOR," SAID WALTER PARKES.

BELOW MIDDLE
WILL SMITH (AGENT JAY) WAS AN UP-AND-COMING TV COMEDIAN WHEN THE SHOOTING STARTED FOR *MEN IN BLACK*. TODAY, HE'S YOUR BASIC INTERNATIONAL SUPERSTAR WITH ACTION PICTURES LIKE *INDEPENDENCE DAY* AND "SERIOUS" FILMS LIKE *ALI* TO HIS CREDIT. AND HE'S STILL A NICE GUY.

BELOW RIGHT
RIP TORN (ZED). MORE THAN A HUNDRED FILMS TO HIS CREDIT, AND HE'S STILL GOING STRONG.

DAVID CROSS (NEWTON). We didn't even know what his name was in the original film. He was just the morgue attendant who got glued to the ceiling by Edgar Bug's spittle, a can of insect repellent still clutched in his hand. But contrary to appearances, that character—played by actor David Cross—wasn't dead. Apparently, the MIB Hazmat guys got to him in time, got him down, cleaned him up, and sent him on his way. Now he returns, with a name and a new job and a room of his own (in his mom's house, it seems). Cross is a busy character actor, and has been since the mid-1990s. He was half of "Mr. Show" in the cult TV program of the same name, and has appeared in such wildly variant work as *Waiting for Guffman*, *The Truth About Cats and Dogs*, and *Ghost World*.

ALPHEUS MERCHANT (SECURITY GUARD). This is the level of commitment exhibited by *Men in Black II*. *This* is how important continuity is to the film. Because even the bored old security guard, the one down in the MIB lobby, makes a return appearance. Same guy, same place, same *chair*. Because *MIB* isn't just a franchise. It's a *world*...and Alpheus Merchant is its guardian at the gate.

The New Ones

Meanwhile, three new characters are central to the story of *Men in Black II*:

LARA FLYNN BOYLE (SERLEENA). Lara Flynn Boyle *(Twin Peaks, The Practice)* was brought in to take on the role of the impossibly sexy, impossibly evil Kylothian monster-queen.

"She was amazing," Walter Parkes said. "The way she just came in. She had to deal with prosthetics and special effects, and she had to do everything with an almost pitch-perfect comic timing...and she did."

Though Boyle appeared in a few films in the late 1980s, her big break was certainly David Lynch's *Twin Peaks* television series in 1990. As Donna Hayward, she struck a haunting chord as an intelligent, sexy, and slightly spooky character. She reinforced that in some wonderfully cultish classics—*Red Rock West* and *The Temp*, among others—and eventually landed on ABC's *The Practice* as Assistant District Attorney Helen Gamble, where she supplies an intelligence and sexuality that can't be ignored. Serleena is all that and *much* more—a murderous alien in the body of a Victoria's Secret model, who delivers some of the funniest and *meanest* lines in the film while flailing thorny neural roots and morphing into a whole series of Monsters of the Id.

"She was as much fun as Will," Stephanie Kemp said. "From day one, she came in laughing and full of energy. She was gleefully evil and she *loved* it."

JOHNNY KNOXVILLE (SCRAD/CHARLIE). Knoxville was brought on board by Barry Sonnenfeld. "I had a great time working with him on *Big Trouble*," Sonnenfeld said. "So when I read this part, I knew it was right for Johnny." Born Phillip John Clapp—which may explain the name change—in Knoxville, Tennessee, Johnny was working for a skateboarding magazine when he wrote a story about self-defense equipment that he tested on himself. That attracted the attention of the Right People, and after a bidding war between Comedy Central and MTV...there was *Jackass*. Not that he lacks formal training. Johnny is a graduate of the respected American Academy of Dramatic Arts; he was even offered a spot on *Saturday Night Live* at one point, though he turned it down. And that may have been a good idea: Not only is he a celebrity in his own right with *Jackass*, and not only does he have two major pictures coming out within months of each other in 2002...he's already signed with Amblin for another project, *Big Ticket*.

ROSARIO DAWSON (LAURA VASQUEZ). In a movie—actually a pair of movies—with virtually no romance to speak of, Rosario Dawson stands out as the single Romantic Interest...even though Laura and Jay share only a single kiss. Dawson, who made a big splash in 2001 as Valerie in *Josie and the Pussycats*, was literally "discovered" while sitting on the stoop in front of her Manhattan apartment, and cast in the harsh semidocumentary *Kids* at the tender age of sixteen. A few years later, Spike Lee saw something impressive in her, as well, and cast her in *He Got Game*. Then

BELOW RIGHT
JOHNNY **K**NOXVILLE (SCRAD/CHARLIE). "A RIOT...HE WILL GO OVER THE TOP IF HE HAS TO—HE'S READY TO DO IT, ABLE TO DO IT, WILLING TO DO IT—AND HE DOES," SAYS STEPHANIE KEMP.

BELOW LEFT
ROSARIO **D**AWSON (LAURA). THE EARTH-MOTHER ANGEL IN A COMPANY OF CUTUPS; EXACTLY AS WARM AND FRIENDLY AS SHE SEEMS.

came a variety of other roles in small pictures, then *Josie*, and *Men in Black II*. Yet Dawson remains the sweet and warm young woman she was back on those New York steps. "As gleefully evil as Lara Flynn Boyle was," Stephanie Kemp recalled, "Rosario was the lovely earth mother to everybody. Her mom was around all the time, cooking stuff for people. She was great. Rosario is the kind of person you greet in the morning, and get a big kiss on the cheek, and then you just *have* to be nice all day. That's what she instills."

"It's the A Team," Walter Parkes said, and he meant both in front of the camera and behind it.

Twelve and a Half Weeks, MIB-Style

"Bob Gordon did two significant drafts," Marc Haimes recalled of the script process. "Drafts that everyone loved and empowered the project in a big way."

By then, Barry Sonnenfeld was on board, and he wanted to move forward very closely with a writer of his own. He chose Barry Fanaro, with whom he had worked happily on *Big Trouble*. "Everyone was happy with it," Haimes said. "Barry Fanaro had a smart problem-solving mind, and brought a lot to the project in terms of his comedy. He opened up the project just a little bit more."

There was reshuffling of scenes, a honing of ideas. The sense of humor of the movie was broadened. "He brought more 'pop culture' to the movie," Haimes said, "which Gordon completely avoided, very deliberately. The structure got a lot tighter under Fanaro...but a lot stayed with that script from the very first draft."

The producers and the new director worked closely together for the next twelve weeks, with help from a wide variety of others, including Haimes and Fanaro. The goal was to create a complete structure, a real shooting script, that Barry Sonnenfeld could run with. They had the great advantage of knowing what they wanted and where they were going. They all loved the first film; they all wanted more of the same, only better.

"You know, you get Barry Sonnenfeld on one side, and the two of us on the other," said Walter Parkes, "and…there's not a lot of compromise. But that's a good thing; that makes us all work harder. That period of time is fascinating, difficult, and ultimately great. It's a hard road you travel to get there, but once that's over—once we got into about the third day of shooting—we were all very happy."

"I really think my major role is to set a *tone*," Barry Sonnenfeld commented. "It's really nothing more than that."

"What he's saying is absolutely true," Walter Parkes agreed, "but it's a complicated and difficult thing to maintain the tone on a movie like this. There are a lot of people who could direct it, but they would become so overwhelmed by the visual effects or the physical special effects or just the sheer size of it that the first thing they would lose would be that *tone*."

And that wasn't going to happen. Not on a Barry Sonnenfeld set.

Get Ready for Action!

Barry Sonnenfeld had a reputation for and a commitment to keeping a happy, loose set. He did that in part by bringing in the right people—people he liked and could trust—then giving them the chance to be involved in the actual making of the picture.

"Barry Sonnenfeld is on every page of this script," Walter Parkes said. "Bo Welch is on every page. Rick Baker is on every page. Tommy Lee Jones and Will Smith are on every page. They all had a tremendous amount to do with crafting the final product."

Everybody was part of the process. Tony Shalhoub improvised most of his lines for the Jeebs

> …AND THIS IS WHY THEY *REALLY* CAME BACK. ACCORDING TO ASSOCIATE PRODUCER STEPHANIE KEMP, "YOU'RE WORKING HUGE DAYS, BUT EVERYBODY HAD WORKED TOGETHER SO MANY TIMES, THERE WERE NO GAMES, NO TESTING, VERY FEW POLITICS. NONE OF THAT. IT WAS FUN. EVEN THE DAYS THAT WEREN'T SUPPOSED TO BE FUN WERE FUN."

ABOVE RIGHT
BARRY SONNENFELD
ATTEMPTING TO EXPLAIN WHAT WAS
SUPPOSED TO HAPPEN DURING THE
CLIMACTIC "ROOFTOP/SERLEENA"
SCENE NEAR THE END OF *MIB II*.
"THERE'S THIS BIG MONSTER, SEE,
THAT USED TO BE A VICTORIA'S
SECRET MODEL, AND SHE'S GOING
TO THRASH YOU WITHIN AN INCH OF
YOUR MISERABLE LIFE." SMALL
WONDER THE BOYS IN BLACK ARE
LOOKING A LITTLE WORRIED.

ABOVE
TOMMY TAKES HIS WORM
FOR A WALK. THE WORM GUYS
AREN'T EVEN *IN* THIS SCENE, BUT
NOTHING STOPS THEM FROM
TAGGING ALONG.

basement scene; Will Smith was key in making the relationship between Jay and Laura work as well as it did, without overt love scenes or a whole lot of time. Johnny Knoxville and Lara Flynn Boyle both transformed their roles—and, to a degree, rewrote parts of the movie—with their own suggestions and improvisations.

"When you have a strong direction," Parkes said, "when everybody knows where you're going and agrees on how to get there, you can open things up like that. You can keep things loose."

That was Sonnenfeld's plan, and it worked. "I just believe in surrounding myself with people who are more intelligent than I am," he said, "and letting them do their job. Then I look good, and they get to do what they want."

To top it all off, there was Will Smith. He seemed dedicated to the proposition of making people laugh, and he succeeded every single day. "He has certain characters he does on set," Stephanie Kemp remembered. "He had one guy who was Graham Place's overzealous assistant. His only job was to save money for 'Mr. Graham Place.' He was the favorite one, I think, but he had a bunch of them. And then, of course, he has his posse of guys who have been with him for a long time. They just keep everybody going.

Will Smith's relationship with Tommy Lee Jones extended far beyond the shoot. Many days, they would sit on the edge of the soundstage and talk at length. Smith and Sonnenfeld would start their morning banter, and Jones would occasionally interject some comment or retort. "Tommy's very dry," Kemp noted. "He's a man of few words…which was interesting in this group, because there aren't a lot of us like that."

Finally, all was ready. Financing was set. The studio was committed. The stars were on board.

Barry had a workable script in his hands, and his creative team, headed by Bo Welch and Rick Baker, was in place. It was *his* movie now…his and Graham's and Tommy's and Will's and everybody else's.

Time to get started.

DOSSIER

#7037

To: Alien Tracking
          MBI Office 4-018-5
From: Field Agent O, Hollywood Division
Subject: Cinovation Hidden Complex

It doesn't look like much. Not from the *outside*, anyway.

Cinovation, Rick Baker's monster factory in Glendale, California, is absolutely nondescript: a big, windowless building in the industrial-park neighborhood, with no signs out in front to tell you what lurks inside.

The lobby is much the same: a long Formica countertop, a series of small offices, well kept but far from unusual. You have to look twice to notice that the posters in the waiting area are of the famous monsters of filmland, and the photographs behind the counter were taken at the Academy Awards ceremony last year...and the year before that, and the year before *that*.

If you get past the front counter and stay downstairs, you'll find a very clean, very well-organized series of rooms that resemble a well-run biomedical facility—you know, the places where they develop and build prosthetic limbs or surgical equipment. Again, you have to look twice, and in the corners, to see anything unusual. Like that cardboard box next to the conference table. Isn't that a *tentacle* sticking out of it? And that little sculpture sitting on the counter by the coffee. That's...that's a *hand*.

It's a bit of a maze back there.

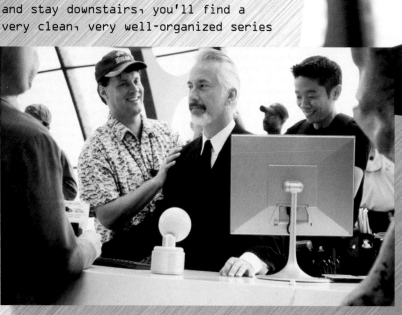

Rick Baker attempting to be a Man in Black. Frightening potential! To his right is Kazuhiro Tsuji, chief makeup aritst and designer for Cinovation. To his left is Jeff Murrell, chief lighting technician.

Rick Baker as a toothy alien during Serleena's takeover of MIB HQ. He entered and exited unnoticed.

If you're lucky, and you're here to actually meet Rick Baker himself, you'll get led upstairs. Down *this* corridor, and around *that* corner; through *this* door and then up a curving staircase to the second floor...

...and everything changes. Suddenly the walls are faux marble. (Or maybe it's *not* faux. How can you tell?) You turn again and you're confronted by a series of tall carved wooden doors. It takes a good shove to open those, or have them opened for you...

...and then you enter the castle of Frankenstein.

These are Rick Baker's private quarters. This is the sanctum where he dreams up the creatures that haunt all our dreams. And it is *exactly* the kind of place you'd expect it to be.

It's a series of four high-ceilinged rooms, connected by high carved archways, and it really *does* look like a castle. There are richly patterned rugs thrown over the slate floors; the furniture is heavy and well padded; the lighting is indirect but pervasive.

You're standing in the conference room, the meeting area. A series of deep couches and chairs surrounds a low wooden table. Off to the left, through one of the arches, is a display room. Three of its rooms are filled top to bottom with shelves, and there are heads sitting on those shelves—*hundreds* of heads. Monsters. Aliens. Gorillas. Old people. *Creatures*, for lack of a better term.

These are all Rick Baker's lifework, and they are beautiful and lovingly maintained. There's no dust in here. Nothing is cramped. It's cool and very quiet—you can't hear the rumble of traffic outside, or the hum of the workers one floor below.

A huge portrait of a white gorilla is mounted on the wall in front of you, just to the left of another wide, high arch. If you were to go in there, you'd find two work areas: a fully equipped computer station, with all the latest in input devices, monitors, and printers on one side, and an equally well-appointed studio for sculpture or carving on the other side.

And then you get to meet Rick. He's

Rick Baker confers with John Berton and Susan Greenhow of ILM.

a surprisingly handsome guy, with a closely cropped white beard and a dark generous mustache that has yet to turn color. His hair is very long, well past his shoulders, but pulled back in a tight salt-and-pepper pony-tail. He has a gold earring and a firm handshake, and he puts you at ease right away.

You might want to say, "You don't look like a geek!" but the thing is, you've read a number of interviews where Baker has called himself exactly that—a makeup geek.

You talk about *Men in Black* for a few minutes. You have a little lunch. You ask him about the rumors that he was thinking of quitting, and he nods. "A couple of years ago, I was ready to close up," he said. "We had just wrapped *Nutty Professor 2—The Klumps* and *How the Grinch Stole Christmas*, which we were filming simultaneously, and I was tired. I really wanted to spend time with my family." But then he got a call from Tim Burton, who had finally cleared the decks and was ready to do the

remake of *Planet of the Apes*. Burton knew there was nobody—*nobody*—who could do it justice but Rick Baker.

"So..." he said, "...I took it on." It was a huge project—the biggest he'd ever attempted, and Cinovation is always involved in the *big* projects. But before it ended, he got a call from Ron Howard, who told him all about *How the Grinch Stole*

Bart Mixon of Cinovation supervising the alien autopsy.

Christmas...and he started thinking about Whoville and the Whos, and what he could do with that.

Now he's worked out a compromise. He takes more time off. He goes home on time and works there when he can. The marathon sessions at the office or on location have been reduced dramatically. But there always seems to be another cool project—like *Men in Black II*—that keeps him interested.

Nowadays he comes in only when there's something to do. He'll spend the first couple of hours downstairs, working with the crew, going over projects, making sure things are on track with his shop supervisor, Bill Sturgeon. But then, usually by ten in the morning, he heads upstairs and closes his door and tells Heidi Holicker—his right hand and guardian at the gate—to take the calls. And he *works*. He draws, he dreams, he sculpts, he paces. He creates yet another set of monsters.

And you realize that this really *is*

a kind of castle of Frankenstein. This is the place where monsters get made, where life is breathed into constructs of rubber and wood.

What's more, this place—these four rooms, and the complex underneath them—just *might* be the dream of the teenage makeup geek that Rick Baker claims to have been. *When I grow up, that kid may have said, I'm going to have this cool workroom. It's gonna look like a castle, and I'll be able to sit in it every day, for as long as I want, and just create, just do the stuff I really love.*

And it seems to be working. December 2001 was actually the Month of Rick Baker all around America. Every video store in the country had larger-than-life reproductions of *two* Baker creations in the window: Tim Roth in *Planet of the Apes* and Jim Carrey in full Grinch. And this from a guy who's *cutting back*.

You ask him if he's going to keep at it. If the compromises are working, and the projects are still coming in.

"Oh, I'll keep doing it," he says thoughtfully, "as long as it's fun."

Chet Zar, sculptor/painter, works on an early alien design.

BRAVE NEW WORLD

CHAPTER 2

Offscreen Space:
The Final Frontier

"Offscreen space," Associate Producer Marc Haimes called it. "That's the key to the Men in Black universe. If you just look the right way or do the right thing, you'll catch sight of something amazing." It's a world that extends *beyond* the borders of the movie screen; it's a world filled with hidden rooms and secret devices that *almost* look normal…that you can *almost* understand. And it's *everywhere*—it's all around us.

It's that *offscreen space* that most intrigues *MIB* fans—the idea that the commonplace is anything *but* commonplace, that a nondescript municipal building, "seven stories high, gray, windowless, perfectly square, squatting on a bridge over a road like a fat guy on the john," can actually be the home of the most amazing organization in the universe.

What's more, the MIB world has to have an identifiable, slightly otherworldly look all its own—a look that remains consistent in its architecture, interior design, engineering, and even weaponry. Artifacts in the MIB world don't just have to look cool. They have to *be* cool. And what's more, they have to have a reason to exist at all.

Back in the early days of production design for the original *Men in Black*, Bo Welch conceived of a whole back story for the "MIB look."

"As I understand it," revealed Production Artist Francois Audouy, assistant art director for *MIB* and a longtime member of Bo Welch's team, "the Men in Black organization was put together in the Sixties, and that had a lot to do with the initial direction of what everything looks like."

That look still holds true. There's a kind of early James Bond/*Man from U.N.C.L.E.* feel to everything the MIB builds: clean, almost geometric—monumental and unadorned. Welch actually studied and extrapolated from the architecture of the period, paying particular attention to the work of architect Eero Saarinen and contemporary monumental works like the St. Louis Arch and the Chicago Air Terminal. The result is a glimpse of what the future looked like almost forty years ago…and it hasn't been redesigned since.

That, too, is part of the MIB back story: "They really don't change much of anything," Welch noted. "They keep their

As Agent Kay explained in *Men in Black*, "back in the mid-Fifties, the government started a little underfunded agency with the simple and laughable purpose of establishing contact with a race not of this planet. Everybody thought the agency was a joke except the aliens, who made contact on March second, nineteen sixty-one, outside New York." It must have been in 1962–1963, then, that MIB architecture and design were created. Notice the ellipses, reminiscent of flying saucers; the near absence of straight lines; and the dominance of flat black, bright white, and highly polished chrome and silver.

architecture because, quite honestly, they can't be concerned with style. They're too busy. Once it's done, it's done."

And what's more, the MIB world interpenetrates the "real" world in a hundred surprising ways. Wherever you least expect it...there it is. And it's *everywhere.* "Not only do you not know about it," Welch said, "but you have no idea how extensive it is. That's one of the fun ideas—the MIB is *vast.* Its resources are endless."

But for all its fascinating details, the world of the MIB is only one of *two* mythical places that Bo Welch had to conceive and make real. The other was his own personal version of modern-day New York—one that, in every scene, had to look completely *different*, right down to the molecular level, from the MIB world that was hiding inside it.

The Manhattan of *MIB* is no more the "real" New York than MIB Headquarters is a "real" high-tech office. "The idea," Welch said, "is to set up a contrast between the gritty real world of New York—the pizza parlors, video stores, and apartments—and the Men in Black world."

...AND THEN COMES BO WELCH'S VISION OF THE "REAL" WORLD—CLUTTERED, FULL OF "STUFF," AND ALL IN EARTH TONES. EVERY SINGLE DETAIL IS CAREFULLY DESIGNED.

Welch's New York is "smaller, denser, more textured. It has more character, so that you get a good sharp contrast with the neat, clean architectural spaces of the Men in Black.

"The other thing you find," Welch continued, "is that the more cluttered and messy, the more real, but exaggerated, the funnier it is to put two guys in black suits, white shirts, and black ties into it. Again, it's contrast. They look like they *belong* in MIB Headquarters, but in an apartment with a lot of wallpaper...well, they look *funny*. It just makes me laugh. They're completely out of place, and yet they're trying to blend in."

This compare-and-contrast design approach is entirely Bo Welch's invention, too. In the original source material—Lowell Cunningham's comic books—the MIB world looked like "gritty" New York itself. "Originally," Welch said, "the MIB was housed in adjoining brownstones with the common walls taken out. It was filled with typewriters, piles of newspapers, files. An old detective-office kind of look."

That was originally the way Barry Sonnenfeld was going to go, too. "He called me and said, 'I don't know if you even want to do this movie,'" Welch recalled. "'There's not much to do. We're going to shoot realistic in New York.' But still, we wanted to work together, so I said okay...and then I read it, and it occurred to me that it would be fun to inject this whole other *look* into it. I was confident I could sell this idea to Barry—to open up the movie and make it

RIGHT
TIME HAS MOVED ON,
AND SO HAS THE IMMIGRATION
CENTER. NOW IT HAS A STRIP
MALL OF ITS OWN.

BELOW
"**W**E TOOK WHAT WE HAD,"
WELCH SAID, "AND WENT TO THE
NEXT LOGICAL PLACE. HERE,
THINGS HAVE BECOME MORE AND
MORE HOMOGENIZED; CORPORATE
CULTURE HAS BECOME MORE
AND MORE INVASIVE. THE
MIB WOULDN'T BE IMMUNE TO
THAT. SO EVEN IN MIB
HEADQUARTERS, YOU'RE GOING TO
FIND THE SAME STORES YOU FIND
IN OTHER MALLS."

a little more eye-popping. Because it *is* a fun movie, after all."

Sonnenfeld was an easy sell. He latched onto the idea with great enthusiasm, and Welch was very pleased. "It was a concept that enabled you to go top to bottom in designing stuff," he said. And design stuff he did.

He designed offices. He designed furniture. He designed huge machines and handheld gadgets, telephones and forklifts, storage facilities and computers. And guns—tons and tons and *tons* of guns. Ultimately, Bo Welch evolved a whole design vocabulary for the world of the Men in Black, and once you notice it you can't ever ignore it again.

There are ovals everywhere—ovals that represent, if only symbolically, flying saucers. There are very few straight lines. Almost everything is curved into a saucer shape, or into an arch reminiscent of the bowl of the sky itself. Colors are restricted to deep black, bright white, cyan, and silver. No earth tones, and please, *please*, no red or blue. There are no windows—no clashes with the "real" New York around them. And even if the grime of Gotham is crowding outside every exit, everything in the world of the MIB is polished, glittering, *clean*.

Yet in every shot of MIB Headquarters, there's the ubiquitous alien-in-disguise, or an invader who doesn't fit into the mold, looking jarring and, well, *alien* amid the clean, cool continuity of the MIB. Notice, for instance, the scenes in MIB HQ where the loudly dressed Scrad/Charlie is trying to decide whether or not he'll betray Serleena. The contrast is positively *disturbing*.

Accelerated Evolution

Bo Welch's sophisticated conceptual thinking came in particularly handy when he was given the schedule for *MIB II*. The pace of the first film was leisurely compared to the accelerated schedule of the sequel. Only two things allowed him to stay ahead of the game at all: his established "architectural vocabulary," and his time-tested team of artists and designers, virtually all of whom had worked on *MIB*. Tim Flattery, James Carson, and Francois Audouy, among others, all came back as illustrators for *MIB II*, and they all worked night and day right up to the bitter end.

The work began the old-fashioned way. "Pen on paper," Welch revealed. "Then I talked to the illustrators and had them make something prettier with computers or models. Since they had all worked on the first one, I didn't have to back up and say, 'Once upon a time.' I only had to say, 'Remember this? Let's do that...*plus*.'"

"He does these little 'Bo drawings,' we call them," said illustrator Francois Audouy. "On every show, he has a big book that he fills with sketches. We'll take those and create an illustration or a model in Photoshop, then maybe draw on top of that. Then it develops from there. Bo has created these rules for how the Men in Black world looks. It's become the language of the show, and everybody is fluent in it."

TOP
"THE FACT OF THE MATTER IS, THE *ALIENS* LIKE THIS STUFF, TOO."

BOTTOM
AN IDEALIZED VISION OF THE FUTURE: ALIENS FROM ALL OVER THE GALAXY LIVING TOGETHER IN PERFECT HARMONY...AS LONG AS YOU CAN GET WHOPPERS FOR UNDER A BUCK.

It was an odd challenge for Welch. He had worked on sequels before—*Batman Returns* and *Ghostbusters II*—but he'd never worked on a sequel to his *own* work...until now. He had to keep from falling into a "been there, done that" mentality.

"You make it fresh," he said. "At least I already had someplace to start—something that I had already come up with. And it was a world I was anxious to explore further."

Four Steps Forward, One Step Back

Exploration was the key. Poking around in that *offscreen space*. But that meant coming up with new things *and* rethinking the extant designs.

Working together, Sonnenfeld and Welch, along with Rick Baker and other key members of the creative team, came up with more back story. For *MIB II,* it was clear that time had passed—four years, in fact, in MIB-time as well as in "real" time. Even in the relatively unchanging world of the Men in Black, that meant *something.* So what would have changed...and what would have remained the same?

There had been a few major alterations in design implied in the last scene of *Men in Black,* but most of those were quietly forgotten. Maybe Agent Jay had been experimenting with a new design for his sunglasses and a hip black Nehru jacket on that particular day, but clearly he would have been snapped back into place by the sheer inertia of the organization—and by Zed himself—*very* quickly. So back to the Ray•Bans, and back to the bulky 1962 suit. No more talk about the variants.

The exterior of the MIB building wouldn't be touched. Neither would the lobby, or the security guard who sat there thirty-seven hours a day. Furniture designs, computer design, Zed's office—the rule was, don't fix 'em if they ain't broke.

Jay would get one concession, they decided. He *would* get a cooler ride.

Weapons would have to evolve as well. The de-atomizer and the Noisy Cricket would still be around, since after only four years, standard weaponry wouldn't change in the "real" world *or* that of the MIB—but the selection could certainly be expanded. Welch came up with a kind of Noisy Cricket rifle, a two-handed job that brought this powerful, tiny weapon to a new level. And a whole host of new, congruent weapon designs were created.

They would re-dress the gadget room and slightly rearrange the headquarters as well—again, keeping in mind that whatever changes they did make had to be made for a *reason*, and not just to mess with things. The Immigration Center would be the one set that would get the most significant makeover.

"We took what we had," Welch said, "and went to the next logical place. When it came to the terminal, I had to think about our own world. Here, things have become more and more homogenized; corporate culture has become more and more invasive. The MIB wouldn't be immune to that. So even in MIB Headquarters, you're going to find the same stores you find in other malls. The fact of the matter is, the *aliens* like this stuff, too."

The redesign was a clever addition of a strip mall done in the black-and-steel vocabulary of the MIB. There's a Burger King there, with its characteristic slash of red, and a Sprint store. There's even a duty-free shop that features "I ♥ New York" T-shirts. These aliens are *tourists*, after all. Out-of-towners. Why should their hunger for souvenirs be any different from our own?

Every detail of the strip mall had to be translated into MIB designs, so the changes wouldn't look inappropriate or sloppy. Even the most minute graphics, down to the menus and the neon signs, had to be made MIB-specific, including the Burger King typeface and the Sprint store exteriors.

The modifications were done expertly…and what's most astonishing is how *right* it looks. We actually *expect* to see creatures from outer space lounging at Burger King and chomping on Whoppers, cheek to dripping jowl with MIB workers on a break. After all, what's *wrong* with a squat little frog-guy using a dolly to cart away cases of Jack Daniel's? Heck, it's duty-free. He probably got a great deal.

Bo Welch shrugs when he thinks of it now. "This is what we have to offer the universe," he admitted. "Burger King, good long-distance service, and duty-free liquor."

Welcome to Earth. Did you bring your wallet?

BELOW LEFT
THE "OFFICIAL" DENEURALYZER IS A NEAR-PERFECT "MIB MACHINE"—ALL WHITE CURVES AND CHROME GLOBES.

BELOW AND BOTTOM
THE FINAL SET IS VIRTUALLY IDENTICAL TO THE APPROVED RENDERINGS—SO PERFECT, IN FACT, THAT HUMAN FOLKS LOOK ALMOST OUT OF PLACE.

New Places in Old Spaces

Next, there were whole new MIB and New York environments that the script called for—spaces that would have to be developed from scratch. Some of them would never make it past a single draft; others were locked into place from the earliest Gordon scripts and never moved again.

"If it appeared in the script, I designed it," Welch said obligingly…and the result was a whole series of new places that looked as if they'd been there all along—we just hadn't *noticed* them before.

Offscreen Space

Inside MIB HQ, filmgoers will find two major new places:

THE DENEURALYZER ROOM. In some ways, this is Bo Welch's purest MIB design ever: all curves, all ovals, all white and black and chrome. It's essentially a ball suspended inside another ball, the lighting so indirect that the room itself seems to glow, and the overall effect so eerily organic that the arrival of the human Men in Black is jarring—they look angular and out of place. Of course, the design

RIGHT
Shooting switched to a specially dressed-out pool for the near drowning of Agents Jay and Kay.

BELOW
The final version of the "flushing" sequence is pure computer-generated imagery (CGI), sending a virtual Agent Jay shooting through the maze of water pipes and air ducts. Art by Sean Haworth

ELEVATOR SHAFT
INT. MIB H.Q.
S.HAWORTH 3-30-01
MEN IN BLACK 2

serves two purposes: It makes the "official" deneuralyzer look impressive and even a little intimidating…and the curved walls of the room itself make the perfect Giant Toilet Bowl for the unexpected and violent "flushing" sequence that sweeps the agents away before Kay's memory can be restored.

Created on the Sony Pictures Entertainment studio lot, on one of the largest soundstages in existence—the original MGM stage where *The Wizard of Oz* and *Hook*, among many others, were filmed—the set was more like a sculpture than a construct. Lighting it and keeping it clean were small nightmares, and after the first few shots of water, the action moved to a more traditional water tank, dressed to look like the drowned white room.

And one last spooky detail about this particular design is revealed: The final approved rendering of the Deneuralyzer Room is virtually identical to the final, full-sized set, right down to the shape and placement of the individual chrome fixtures—a testament to the skill and attention to detail of *MIB II*'s set construction team.

THE IMPOUND AREA. As an example of *having a reason* for a new set, in both movies, MIB personnel have seized unauthorized space vehicles…but we've never been shown what happened to them. Obviously, they went into

TOP
THE IMPOUND AREA,
ONE OF THE ROOMS SEEN FOR THE
FIRST TIME IN *MIB II*, BEGAN
AS A MUCH CLEANER, MORE
ORGANIZED SPACE…BUT THAT
CHANGED AS TIME WENT ON.

LEFT
THE FINAL IMPOUND SET
WAS A MASTERPIECE OF MESSY,
INTERSTELLAR TRANSPORTATION,
WITH SHIPS FROM EVERY
GENERATION (AND LOTS OF
OTHER MOVIES) CRAMMED
IN EVERY WHICH WAY.

OPPOSITE
Look for homages to...
My Favorite Martian,
Mars Attacks!, and just
about everything in between.

Impound, just like stolen cars recovered by terrestrial cops. Like the robot that always got up on its legs to deliver an answer, *it stands to reason...*

Consequently, the Impound area became a major set for action, where Jay fights Jarra, and Serleena keeps her hideously beautiful Insect Ship.

Early renderings of Impound show a much cleaner and more ordered space than appeared on screen. It's not clear how much of the chaos seen in the final version was a result of the havoc wreaked by Serleena and her cronies, but certainly the more crowded and disorganized approach more closely resembled a typical, "real" Impound lot maintained by Earth-bound law enforcers.

A number of lovingly rendered details skip by in the shots of the Impound. The various interstellar vehicles being kept there were actually borrowed from real-world memorabilia collectors, built from found parts, and purchased from outside vendors of all kinds, to create a kind of jumble-art homage to science-fiction cinema. The adept movie viewer might catch a glimpse of a fully tricked-out Mercury capsule hiding back in the shadows, or a craft that looks strangely familiar and resembles a one-man submarine. That's a full-sized replica of the spaceship from the old TV series *My Favorite Martian,* built by a hobbyist named Steve Stockburger in Anaheim, California. Another ship looks a bit like a space capsule with a living brain attached. *MIB II* crew people added the brain, but the rest of it is an actual capsule mold acquired from aerospace builders General Dynamics. The largest saucer-shaped vehicle is a leftover from *Mars Attacks!,* while two much smaller saucers—the ones on stands—were custom-built by a private company called Modern Props, based in Los Angeles. There's also a glimpse of a large silver ship that looks like something out of Buck Rogers—a ship large enough to actually sit in. That one is a working, running vehicle created by Los Angeles artist Barry Margo.

The ships were acquired through an exhaustive search that involved lots of phone calls, a fair amount of bargaining, and a lot of creative construction and set dressing. All in all, it's a masterpiece created by "the best props department in the business, bar none"—a direct quote from Prop Maker Foreman Peter "Paco" Alvarez.

Out in messy old New York, you'll find Ben's Famous Pizzeria of Soho, the Tapeworm Video Store, Newton's poster-clogged bedroom, and various rooftops and streets, all carefully crafted to fit the earth-toned clutter of Bo Welch's New York. But there are three particular "real-world" environments that straddle the two different worlds in interesting and slightly bizarre new ways:

THE WORM GUYS' BACHELOR PAD. Caught between two eras, this strange and wonderful set went through a number of iterations as drawings and miniatures before it was finally built and dressed. Clearly, the room was supposed to reflect the arrested personalities of the Worm Guys themselves—their shallowness and addiction to popular culture. In this case, the development was *architecturally* arrested, as well—stalled out someplace in the middle of the shag carpet/conversation pit 1970s. Here you'll find a "modern" fireplace and a hot tub, a highly expensive and inefficient exercise machine, an absolutely pointless split-level floor, some of the ugliest lamps and wallpaper ever created, and *really* low ceilings—too low, in fact, for normal humans. And though it doesn't follow the MIB "vocabulary," it's not really part of Bo Welch's New York, either. It's someplace in between...and it's pure *worm*, baby.

JEEBS'S BASEMENT. In another "hybrid" approach, the basement where Jeebs keeps his cobbled-together deneuralyzer is as cluttered as his pure New York upstairs...but it's cluttered with MIB world hardware, at least in part. There are some of the curves and ovals of MIB architecture, iterated in the curved ceiling and

walls—apparently Jeebs's place opens up on an abandoned sewer or subway tunnel—and a ghost of the exquisite "official" deneuralyzer in the curves of the hacked-together amateur unit. But all the earth tones and textures are pure Welch New York…and it gets even worse when Serleena's thugs blow open a wall and open a can of whup-ass.

THE ROCK SCULPTURE ROOFTOP. With its clean lines and cool dark colors, the huge smooth stone sculpture is almost unearthly in its shape. Once again, Welch's two worlds collide: The shapes of the MIB are apparent, but on an open rooftop overlooking the harbor. The set—which was dressed and re-dressed so many times, crew members claim to have lost count—was also built on the Sony lot, and it's *supposed* to have a slightly otherworldly feel to it. It is, after all, the hide-in-plain-sight location of the Light of Zartha's interstellar escape vehicle.

KAY'S OLD APARTMENT. And finally, the viewers' one and only glimpse—so far—into the private life of an MIB agent. It stands to reason: Agents like Jay and Kay must have *someplace* to go when they're not on duty—assuming, of course, they're *ever* not on duty. But an always prepared flat-foot like Agent Kay would also want to be fully armed for any eventuality, even on his home turf. Where a normal cop—or even a normal MIB agent—might settle for a Noisy Cricket in the cupboard, or a Big Blue under the bed, Kay would almost certainly go one giant step further…all the way to a secret room filled with weaponry, hidden behind a cleverly falsified wall.

Since it's been years since Kay left New York City, of *course* the place has long since been rented, by an entirely unsuspecting family. That family, by the way, is a three-way cameo. The dad is Barry Sonnenfeld himself. The mom is Stephanie Kemp, a longtime associate of Place's and Sonnenfeld's who worked on the first *Men in Black* and *Wild Wild West*, among other projects. The daughter is Victoria Jones, Tommy Lee's daughter.

Stephanie Kemp remembered the day of the shoot very well. "Bo had designed this really great, very conservative set, perfect for a couple sitting very properly on the couch, watching Martha Stewart on TV with their coffee-table books and botanical prints surrounding them. But we cast the 'newlyweds,' as the script called them, with two young, urban-looking kids definitely too hip for this apartment. Standing on the set the day before the shoot, Barry comes to a realization and says, 'I think we made a mistake on the casting of the newlyweds. They need to be old and bored. Maybe *I* should do it.' Then, looking at me, he added, 'We could *both* do it.' I looked at him and said, 'Would

THE ROOFTOP SET. THE CREW LOST TRACK OF HOW MANY TIMES THEY HAD TO RE-DRESS THIS SET AS THE DESIGNERS TRIED TO CAPTURE THE PERFECT BALANCE BETWEEN THE MEN IN BLACK AND THE WORLD WE KNOW.

OPPOSITE
That's Victoria Jones
(Tommy's daughter), Director
Barry Sonnenfeld, and
Associate Producer Stephanie
Kemp as the family who
innocently took up residence
in Kay's old apartment...and
had no idea there was a
whole roomful of intergalactic
weaponry right behind the
floral lithographs.

it still start with a kissing scene?' and he said, 'Oh, no, we wouldn't do that.' That was how it happened."

The scene was shot in a single afternoon in about half a dozen takes. Sonnenfeld's only direction to his "wife" and "child": "Don't do anything. Just sit there."

Although the day went pretty well...Kemp admitted that, "the dailies were the most painful thing I've ever sat through in my life."

Lost but Not Forgotten

The ever-changing nature of the *Men in Black II* script—like *MIB* before it—combined with the collapsed preproduction schedule to force the creation of a few fascinating environments that never got beyond the conceptual or model stage.

THE MORGUE. In the early days, when Agent Elle was still a part of the story, the script called for an MIB morgue to be created. This variant stayed around long enough for a full set of renderings to be prepared, and a miniature to be built. Bo Welch and his team even added a rendering of the multilimbed dead alien that was being autopsied at the time—the one that Elle would be crawling around—and through—for most of her scenes.

It was a pretty impressive space: high steel walls on all four sides, dramatic conical lighting, and the biggest autopsy table in the world. But the really disturbing—or maybe *funny*—element was to be the doors in the walls. In a normal, human morgue, they're all the same size. Human beings, after all, fall into a pretty narrow range of dimensions. But in the MIB morgue, the doors were to have been wildly different sizes, from tiny chipmunk drawers all the way up to small garage doors. And you have to wonder what the *heck* is lying on *those* slabs.... .

When Elle disappeared, so did the morgue...though the Big Dead Alien turned out to have a life of its own. It was simply moved into the MIB lobby, to become another quirky detail that somehow makes the whole place more believable.

THE ALIEN STRIP CLUB. In Gordon's initial drafts, Kay's deneuralyzation comes at a different, later point in the script...and his actual recovery of memories comes at an even *later* point.

"Nothing happened for several scenes after the deneuralyzation," Marc Haimes explained. "They just keep going ...and the fight scene that now happens at Jeebs's place actually took place at an alien strip club." In that version, Agents Jay and Kay went undercover—they put on alien drag—to get into a club patronized exclusively by extraterrestrials. "Tentacles and the whole thing," Haimes said. "Kay gets to a special room—Booth Nine—where there is the most hideous stripper of all. She remembers him very well. She says, 'Oh, Kay, we were so great together,' and he has *no* recollection of this. Then the thugs show up, and Kay recovers his memory during the fight as Jay is getting beaten up. He saves Jay, and later realizes that the stripper has slipped him a matchbook while the fight was going on, which leads them to the next place they go."

Ultimately, however, the early designs for the strip club didn't please anyone, and Sonnenfeld and Fanaro decided to have the deneuralyzation happen much earlier in the script—in Jeebs's basement.

Interestingly, both *MIB* and *MIB II* had scenes with humans dressed as aliens...and in both cases, the scenes never made the final cut. "No one else may remember this," Marc Haimes said, "but I thought it was great. In *Men in Black*, Jay and Kay chase Edgar into a science-fiction convention, where they run into all these humans dressed up as aliens. Here they are, running through the convention, trying to trap aliens dressed as humans, but being impeded by humans dressed as aliens." Here, too, it didn't work all that well, and the scene was rewritten. Still, don't be surprised if somewhere during *Men in Black III* you see some principal characters getting all decked out in alien drag. Some ideas, it seems, just *never* die...

AUDOUY
INT. MIB MORGUE

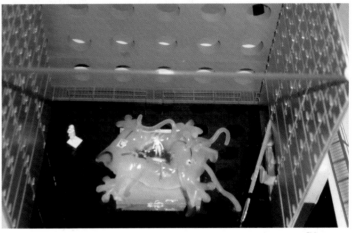

THE MORGUE MADE IT THROUGH THE RENDERING AND MODEL PHASE, BUT NO FURTHER. WHAT WOULD BE HIDING ON THE SLABS BEHIND THOSE DOORS? ART BY FRANCOIS AUDOUY

DOSSIER

#1663

To: **Managing Director W**
           Lost & Found Department
           Civilizations Division
           MIB Office 2-734-8
From: **Collator and Replicator Q**
Subject: **Secrets of Grand Central**
           Terminal

WELCOME TO LOCKERTOWN.
ADULT SECTION IN THE BACK!

Lockertown: Hidden in a most unexpected place, forgotten for twenty-five years, populated by a nameless alien race that worships Agent Kay. Hiding place of great secrets, home to the smallest red-light district on Earth.

Lockertown: It's only on screen for a very short time, but there's no doubt about it—the tiny little burg, with people as diminutive as lice, is a fascinating place.

It began almost as a throwaway concept—one of many, many props that the *MIB II* script required. But it turned into a major undertaking—"one of those things," Stephanie Kemp remembered, "that seems simple but never ends."

Set Designer Kevin Ishioka is a little more charitable. He, along with Art Director Tom Wilkins and Set Designers John Chichester and Will Hawkins, labored extensively on Lockertown. "It developed in many different ways as various people worked on it. I did a lot of the shopping for all the stuff that would be in it, from a whole lot of different places. Then we just started...well, making buildings."

As the town took shape, the appar-

ently random collection of objects acquired a remarkably charming look. Coffee cans, shampoo bottles, dead dry-cell batteries, matchbooks, and a hundred other items were all crafted into quaint little houses and storefronts, temples with winding staircases, even a town square with a fountain. It somehow acquired a pleasant, old-fashioned feeling—almost soothing.

The original flooring was a mess of nasty, torn-up newspaper, but that was "too much," said Ishioka. "It was too hard to see the buildings, so we decided on a greener background." Model Maker Jason Mahakian was brought in and charged with "pulling it all together, giving it a more green, New England look."

In the final analysis, however, Lockertown belongs to all people: Almost everybody—cast, crew, production staff—had a hand in its construction.

"It's like a dog walking by a fire hydrant," Ishioka remembered. "Everyone had to touch it, had to offer an opinion. 'You know, this building really would be better over here.' That's why we finally let Jason have the final say. Somebody had to...and God knows, he definitely raised it up another notch."

Then the changes started coming down from Welch and Sonnenfeld. "Suddenly we had to have a red-light district at the back," Ishioka recalled...so everything got moved around again. "Then Barry wanted more people in there, so we started scaling back and putting in a city. Now it looks as if there's a vil-

lage in the foreground and a city where you can imagine there are five or ten thousand people."

Stephanie Kemp said, "We thought building it was just going to be great fun...but it didn't end. They made the town, and they made the town, and they *made* the town again...and then the director made a simple basic comment—which he is more than entitled to make:

"'It's too red.'"

Even now, Kemp couldn't help but moan. "Do you know what that does? It's unbelievable."

Work (and reworking) continued

Lockertown in all its splendor. Locker C-18 is off to the left, giving a sense of just how small this prop really was—and it was this small: no blue-screen or optical effects here, just a good old-fashioned miniature.

TOP LEFT: An earlier incarnation of Lockertown. Notice the lack of vegetation and the "nasty old newspaper" that served as the floor. This led to the mandate: more green, less red, more plants.

DOSSIER

Lockertown aliens in front of a blue-screen, complete with their exotic footwear.

Rick Baker adjusts the hairy little chin-chin-chin of Jane Oshita, one of the lead Lockertowners.

throughout May, June, July, and August for all four crew members and their endless supply of "helpers." "Sometimes we'd stop and go work on another model," Ishioka said, "and then they'd have another opinion, and we'd go back in. If one person had worked on it alone, it would have taken six months."

Finally the Powers That Be—the true Gods of Lockertown—called a halt. The tiny set was carefully lit, and close-up plate shots, with a lot of detail, were taken. A simple motion-control camera rig filmed some dolly shots through the streets of the tiny Lockertown as well.

Even as the micro-city-state of Lockertown struggled to be born, there was an equally painful amount of back-and-forth involving the evolution of its inhabitants. "They just couldn't agree on a Lockertown alien design," Kemp said. "These particular aliens were supposed to be warm and fuzzy

and cute—really, really cute." The final look, after countless attempts, did achieve warm and fuzzy, but with spooky eyes.

Once the design was finally and fully approved by all parties, Cinovation had to create almost a dozen separate suits for the charac-ters. This wasn't going to be a CG effect; from the very beginning, it was all costumes and blue-screen.

Erstwhile Stunt Master Charlie Croughwell as the Moses of the Lockertown aliens.

"Shooting that was incredibly tedious," Kemp said. "You've got these tiny, narrow women dressed up in Yak suits as the Lockertown aliens, and all they do for twelve hours a day—on a hot, empty soundstage, in front of a blue-screen with nothing to look at—is chant, 'Praise Jay! Praise Jay! Praise Jay!'" She shuddered.

The High Priest of the Lockertown aliens was dubbed "Moses," for obvious reasons: He brought the sacred writing—the Tapeworm Video Store card—down from the mountain and interpreted for his people. The actor inside the "Moses" suit was none other than Stunt Coordinator Charlie Croughwell. "Those outtakes are great," Kemp recalled. "Here's the holiest guy in town fumbling his lines, then swearing like a longshoreman as he stomps back up the stairs to do it again."

Months of model-making and days of shooting finally came together in one of the more memorable and unexpected images for *MIB II*...and after all that work, at least somebody got something special out of it:

"The Art Department looked like a junkyard," Stephanie Kemp said. "Here we have this great, high-concept movie...and our Art Department is filled with dead batteries, light-bulbs, matchboxes—junk. One day I went into all that junk, just for kicks, and I saw this little green plaid skirt. I said, 'What is this here for?' and Tom Wilkins said, 'Oh, it's a pattern that might look nice as grass.' I said, 'Oh, no, this would be terrible grass.' Tom very diplomatically countered with, 'Well, let's at least see if Bo likes it.'"

EVERYONE OLD IS NEW AGAIN

CHAPTER 3

"We knew from the beginning," said Marc Haimes, "we wanted more Frank, we wanted more Worm Guys." Together, they represented two of the returning characters who had changed and grown for the sequel...or at least revealed more of themselves.

From the Newsstand to the Executive Suite

"I'm not really a dog," Frank told Jay at one point in *Men in Black*. "I just play one on your planet." Exactly what Frank *is* remains an open question. Is he an alien in a dog suit, like Mikey and Mr. Gentle and so many before him? Or is he an alien in the full flesh who just *happens* to look like an earthly canine?

Whatever Frank's true form, audiences discover that he's gone through a series of career changes in his last few years here on Earth. When they first encountered him in *MIB*, he was hanging out with a gaunt, silent fellow at a typical Manhattan newsstand, sporting a doggy-sized "I ♥ New York" sweatshirt and a real attitude. At the time, Agent Kay described him as "a professional—someone with years of experience in intergalactic politics" and "a little prick," almost in the same breath. Later, after Frank was interrogated by the MIB, Zed revealed that Frank had left the planet in anticipation of its destruction. So had just about every other alien on Earth.

Obviously, Frank—like the Worm Guys and many other fair-weather allies—skulked back to New York, once the Arquillians took their little galaxy and went peacefully home.

But apparently his gig at the newsstand was no longer available. So now, four years later, he's working in the MIB mailroom and looking to get a leg up, so to speak. It's clear he's been waiting for his big break for quite a while—he's had a doggy-sized black suit all tailored up and has it ready and waiting. But he doesn't survive as Jay's partner for long, not with Kay back in the picture.

Nonetheless, Frank rebounds quickly, and by the end of the day he's settled into a new position that seems custom-made for him: executive assistant to Zed himself, where he can use his vast knowledge of interstellar politics, and still get a decent health plan.

It may come as a shock to jaded special-effects fans to discover that Frank the Pug isn't a puppet, nor is he a Baker animatronic, and he's not a computer-generated Industrial Light & Magic effect. He's a *dog*—actually, one of a group of virtually identical pugs that were trained for months to do the things Frank was required to do. The only special effect, other than his nifty little costumes, is the animation of his mouth—an effect supplied by ILM.

- He delivers mail, clutched in his mouth
- He rides in a supersonic Mercedes-Benz, though he did get to stick his head out the window
- He smokes a cigar
- He wears a telephone headset
- He wears a custom-tailored Men in Black suit
- He converses with worms
- He hides in the remains of a huge latex alien

…and he still comes up smiling. Well, not exactly *smiling*. Dogs can't really *smile*, now, can they?

THE MANY FACES OF FRANK THE PUG...

Guys, We Hardly Knew Ye

The film careers of the Worm Guys began with what was essentially a one-line joke: a quick way to convince new recruit James Edwards that there really *were* aliens living on Earth. But their two short scenes in *Men in Black* made the Worm Guys the international celebrities they always knew they deserved to be, and everyone from top to bottom *knew* that they had to make an appearance in the sequel.

It turned out to be much more than an "appearance," though. The four—wait, six—no, eight—no…

Anyway, the ever-increasing ranks of Worm Guys became *major* players in *MIB II*, appearing as guardians for Laura Vasquez—not very *good* guardians, mind you, but *still*—and surprisingly effective commandos.

Far from the days when they were just slackers, hanging around MIB HQ and guzzling coffee, they've been given their own swingin' bachelor pad. They work out, they play Twister. And when forced to, they put on the rig and go all Rambo on you.

They also display a horrifying yet potentially quite useful ability that no one suspected before: If one of the little buggers is cut in half, what you get is *two* little buggers.

What's more, in *Men in Black II* the worms actually have *names*—at least the four "original" ones do. There's Sleeble… and Geeble. There's Neeble… and Mannix. One of them lifts weights. One of them digs TV. They all smoke like chimneys and drink like fish, and they all want to make time with Laura Vasquez. And anyone who says he can tell them apart is lying.

The Worm Guys were a Rick Baker/Cinovation creation—a series of latex puppets mounted on metal armatures, manipulated by puppeteers using a series of rods attached to their joints. ILM

BELOW
SLEEBLE, CATCHING UP ON REQUIRED READING (OR MAYBE THAT'S GEEBLE…).

BELOW RIGHT
NEEBLE, PAUSING FOR A REFRESHING SMOKE (OR IS THAT MANNIX?).

OPPOSITE
AND OF COURSE GEEBLE ALWAYS LIKES TO GET IN HIS REPS.

BOTTOM LEFT
"**I** AM BUT HALF A WORM." THE GUYS' AMAZING ABILITY TO REGROW THEMSELVES FROM EITHER END COMES IN HANDY WHEN THEY NEED A FEW EXTRA BODIES.

BELOW
FULL-BODY WORM PUPPETS APPEAR IN THE "COMBAT" SCENES, SEAMLESSLY INTERSPERSED WITH ILM'S COMPUTER VERSIONS OF THE CHARACTERS.

RIGTH
IT DOESN'T MATTER HOW HAPPY LAURA (ROSARIO DAWSON) LOOKS...THERE'S SOMETHING DEEPLY DISTURBING ABOUT THIS PHOTOGRAPH.

BELOW
THE WORM GUYS' "REALITY" BEGAN WITH RICK BAKER'S REMARKABLE DESIGNS AND HIGHLY RESPONSIVE PUPPETS...BUT THEY TRULY CAME TO LIFE IN THE HANDS—AND AT THE ENDS OF THE STICKS—OF MASTER PUPPETEER TONY URBANO AND HIS CREW.

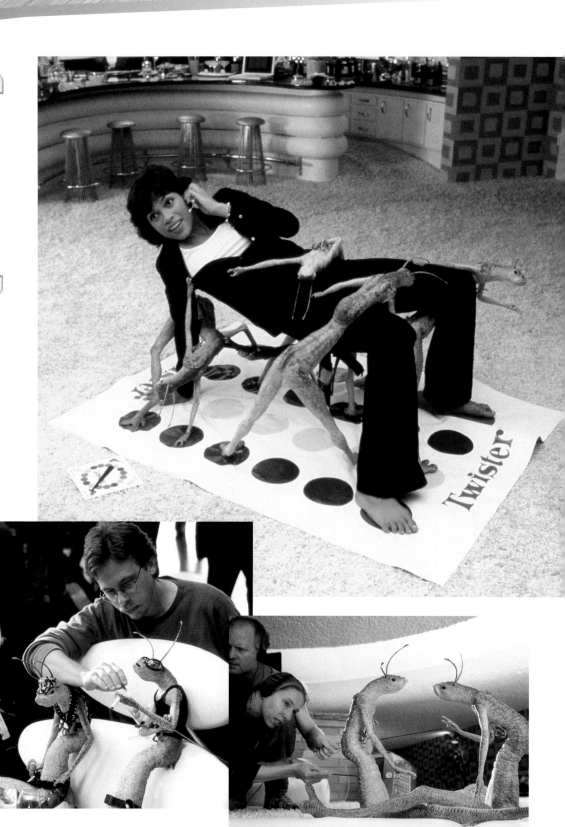

special-effects magicians remove the rods and any other extraneous equipment that might reveal the manipulation, but the real magic comes from the work of the puppeteers themselves, led by Puppet Master Tony Urbano, who also worked closely with Johnny Knoxville on the Scrad/Charlie characterizations.

Once Sleeble, Geeble, Neeble, and Mannix—*is* he named after the detective? no one knows—armor up and head out to take back MIB Headquarters, they *really* start moving. And at that point, some of the scenes involving full-body movement were produced as full CG (computer-generated) effects rather than as puppets. This is just as in *Men in Black*, where shots of the worms walking, running, or stealing cigarettes were produced by ILM, as well.

ILM Visual Effects Supervisor John Berton put together a team that used data gathered during the first film, as well as extensive new references, to create absolutely faithful digital reproductions of the puppets. The team based each Worm Guy's animation on characteristic movements made by the puppeteers, so the switch from latex to pixels and back again would be virtually seamless.

"The worms are so masterfully puppeteered by Tony Urbano and his group that they have characteristics transcending the idea that they're puppets," Berton said. "You can look at them and say, 'Okay, they look a bit puppetish, but then they're *aliens*, and that's the way those aliens are. We really drew on that, and tried to build our computer-graphics creatures so that their tone is the same as the puppets'." When the two technologies work closely together, the switch back

ABOVE
"I'M A *WORM*,
DAMN IT!
WHAT'S YOUR EXCUSE?"

and forth can be seamless, and can actually make both effects more convincing. "We can use our advantages in CGI to have them run across a football field or climb through ventilation shafts and have hand-to-hand battles with other CG creatures—things that are a little beyond the capabilities of the puppeteers. But the reality of the latex puppet is greater than the reality of the computer-graphics image. The puppets' textures, how they read photographically, can give credibility to the CG creatures…and having the CG creatures running around gives credibility to the performance of the puppets. That way, when they're standing still, it appears that they're standing still because *it's time for them to stand still*, not because they're puppets, and puppets can't move that way."

Man of Action

Finally, there's Zed. Zed the Man. Zed the Leader. Zed the *Hero*.

What prepares a man to lead an organization like the MIB? Years of experience? Sure. A superior intellect? Of course. Remarkable powers of observation and deduction? You bet.

ZED CONFIRMS EVERYONE'S SUSPICIONS, AND KICKS BUTT. PAY NO ATTENTION TO THOSE CABLES; THEY WILL MAGICALLY DISAPPEAR (INDUSTRIAL LIGHT & MAGICALLY) BEFORE THE FINAL CUT.

Remember how he just *knew* when to get out of the way of that hurtling globe in *Men in Black ?*

But one other characteristic is terribly important—maybe more important than all those other qualities put together.

You have to be able to kick ass when it's needed.

During the horrible siege of MIB HQ, Zed reveals that he's more than capable of pulling his weight in the mayhem department. First, he withstands the tortures of Serleena—a villainess who nearly killed him twenty-five years earlier—and spits in her eye. Then, given the slightest opportunity, Zed literally leaps into action and gives viewers just a glimpse of how and why he became the Boss of All Bosses in this galaxy's single greatest police force.

He leaps. He kicks. He jumps. He *rocks.*

Now, *that's* an Executive Director.

"Rip was so game," Stephanie Kemp recalled. "We had him hanging upside down and doing karate kicks, and he never complained."

"During Zed's office scenes," Kemp remembered, "they would lift him off the ground on a wire, and he'd do this karate kick at Serleena. Before we could even put him back down on the ground, he'd either still be in character and ready to continue, or he'd be trying not to laugh—and asking Barry to do it one more time."

DOSSIER

#1660

To: Department of Agent Training
From: Curriculum Developer H
Subject: Required Meta-Deduction
          Exercise for All MIB Field
          Personnel

The Key to Kay's Key!
Save the Earth! Win Valuable Prizes!

Like any good MIB agent, Kay always
has a backup plan. Twenty-five years
ago, he wanted to hide the secret of
the Light of Zartha from everyone—
including himself. But before he trig-
gered the self-neuralization that
would seal his memory forever, or at
least for a quarter century, he made
sure to leave a series of clever clues
that only he would fully understand.

Follow the bouncing ball as Agents
Jay and Kay walk the path that leads
to the key, and save the world!

Go To: Ben's Famous Pizzeria of Soho

It's all here waiting for you. All
you have to do is look. Be sure to
bring the picture of Kay pointing
and laughing—it's in your Official
Men in Black Uniform. Look for the
mural with the flying pizzas...or
are those flying saucers? Confirm
your location by checking the awk-
wardly stacked pizza boxes.

Step One: Ben and the Trout

Take a look at the picture of Ben
on a Montauk pier. Is that really
his tuna, or a clever fake? Look at
the background. They don't match at
all.

Step Two: Apply Kay to Fish

Line up your picture of Agent Kay
with the picture of Ben, using
the background as a guide. You
will now find Ben and Kay standing happily together, with Kay
pointing off to his right. Follow
that finger.

Step Three: The "Astronaut"

Warning! This is not a real astronaut! This is Production Designer Bo Welch of *Men in Black II*. Don't be fooled... but follow his pointing finger... .

Step Four: The Pizza Box of Destiny

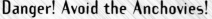

Look at the star. The statue. The slice. Cross your eyes and look at them in a new way. That's not a slice of pizza at all. It is an arrow, indicating your next destination. Follow the pointing pizza... .

Danger! Avoid the Anchovies!

Alignment of pizza points is essential! Do not open cabinet. Do not open can. Do not think of fish. Do not rent boat. Return to the pizza box and try again.

Step Five: The Key to C-18

Take the key hanging next to the original photograph of Ben. It was there all the time. Why didn't you notice it? *GCT* stands for "Grand Central Terminal" not "Greater Connecticut."

Final Note: Find and Retain Napkin!

Special hidden meanings on this translucent tissue could save the world. Do not misplace! Do not destroy! Do not use by mistake when you're looking for a Kleenex!

VERY, VERY GOOD AT BEING VERY, VERY BAD

One thing's for certain: *Men in Black II* sports a lot of bad guys whom fans can really, really *hate*. In fact, there are not one, not two, but *three* major villains who want nothing more than to see the Men in Black destroyed, and Earth reduced to cinders. If you count Scrad/Charlie accurately, it's really more like three and a *half* villains who fill the bill.

Serleena

She's beautiful, she's cruel, and she's definitely not of this Earth. But in fact, Serleena Xath of the planet Jorn in the Kylothian system was the driving force behind the entire film. Even when she wasn't on camera, she was the reason everything happened, from the deneuralyzing of Agent Kay to the near destruction of MIB Headquarters and Jay's strange little voyage of self-discovery.

Serleena's original Kylothian form is hideous, thorny, and entirely computerized. The neural roots that surged from her fingertips—and probably anywhere else she'd like them to surge from—were likewise computer-generated effects produced by Industrial Light & Magic and carefully matched to the live action. But the real power of the character didn't come from her transformative abilities; it came from Lara Flynn Boyle's tough, funny, sexy, *mean* performance.

Over the course of the production, LFB, as she's known to her friends, experienced the opportunity to freeze in her underwear in a California park, stand for hours on end with her arms outstretched, stuff herself with Whoppers, wear a bodysuit that gave her a huge potbelly, and pose as a real live Victoria's Secret model, if only for a day…"and she loved it," noted one coworker.

"There's something brash and Old Hollywood about Lara," Stephanie Kemp said, comparing her favorably to the Grand Old Dames of Hollywood like Joan Crawford and Bette Davis. "Diet Coke, cigarettes, and hamburgers—that was her diet on the show. But she was great. She was up for anything."

Among the most physically demanding shoots were the nocturnal adventures in a Southern California park that doubled as Central Park, Serleena's landing site. During this all-night episode, LFB shot the scenes that would introduce her character: her first moments in human form, the attack by

Creepy the Mugger and his subsequent consumption, and finally her crafting of the trademark bustier she would wear for the rest of the film.

"It was a freezing night in Los Angeles," Stephanie recalled, "and we're shooting at three o'clock in the morning. God love her, she's out there in her little bra and underpants and six-inch heels. She's not shivering, she's not complaining, but in a few of the takes you can see she has goose bumps like sharpened pencils. She'd get inside a cozy little robe between takes and try to warm up, take a hit off her cigarette, throw off the robe, and say, 'Okay, let's do it again!'"

But there was more than just the cold. LFB also had to don a complex and very heavy body-suit that day: one that provided her with a huge false tummy, to explain exactly where Creepy the Mugger had gone. The final effect—that huge belly with the black lace underwear—is stunningly realistic, but the process of getting the thing on and taking it off made for a twenty-hour day, and only a few seconds of very funny film time.

TOP
LARA FLYNN BOYLE
AND HER BUSTIER.

TOP LEFT
JOHNNY KNOXVILLE ENJOYS A
MOMENT WHEN SOMEBODY ELSE IS
GETTING BOTHERED FOR A CHANGE,
AS CINEMATOGRAPHER GREG
GARDINER CHECKS THE DETAILS ON
LARA'S EXACT POSITION, ONE LAST
TIME. FOR ALL ITS SPONTANEITY
AND SPEED, *MIB II*'S SET WAS
A CLASSIC OF MODERN SPECIAL-
EFFECTS FILMMAKING, BEST SUM-
MARIZED BY THE CREW AS "HURRY
UP AND WAIT. A LOT."

ABOVE
FOR ALL THE WORK, WAITING,
AND TEDIUM, LARA FLYNN BOYLE
CLEARLY HAD A GREAT TIME...AND
MADE SURE EVERYONE ELSE DID
THE SAME.

Because of the production schedule, it was more than three weeks after her arrival before she finally got in front of the still cameras to produce the image that was central to her role: the Victoria's Secret spread. The *MIB II* team actually hired fashion photographer Cliff Norton—someone who knew exactly how to capture the look and feel of a *real* VS image—to make Lara look just right. The shoot was long and tedious, but LFB loved every minute of it. Another aspect of the costume pleased her equally: the wonderfully constructed bras that gave a new meaning to the term *push-up*. The real push, however, came from that bustier, a masterpiece of costume design and modern engineering created by Mary Vogt. The abundance of special digital effects that flowed from Serleena

made much of her camera time a challenge. Boyle spent a great deal of time acting to bluescreens, or standing frozen in place while measurements were taken or marker dots were applied to knuckles, elbows, and fingertips. She endured it all with great good humor, and still managed to deliver a wry performance, take after take, that earned her the respect of the entire cast and crew.

Scrad/Charlie

What *is* he, exactly? A Kylothian slave? The last surviving member of some other, previously unsuspected race? Is Charlie—that's the little head, the one that looks like a bad copy of the big head—attached to the main body in some way, or does he live in that backpack? Can he walk? Does he even have *arms*? One shudders to think...but one still wants to *know*.

Actor Johnny Knoxville had to confront all these questions as he built the characters of Scrad and Charlie, and faced the daunting prospect of performing two related roles in the film—that is, finding a way to talk to himself throughout the production, and still be funny.

Charlie and Scrad are an enormously important part of the story line. They certainly took the concept of "talking to yourself" to a whole new and horribly literal level...but more significantly, Charlie and Scrad actually went through a *character arc*, reconsidering the role as minion and lackey, and choosing to save the day—if, perhaps, for all the wrong reasons—at the last moment, saving Jay's life and the Earth in the process.

The performance had to be more than a running joke, then. It had to be an *actual* performance, with an actual character—or a set of characters—about whom audiences would really *care*.

One of the first stars to be attached to the film, Knoxville had already enjoyed one positive relationship with Sonnenfeld on *Big Trouble*. Now he would have to deal with the world of *Men in Black*, and some truly difficult shoots. But he decided he wasn't going to take it slow; he was going to have some *fun* on this picture, and it was going to start the first day.

"It's early in the production," Stephanie Kemp said, "and Johnny's first day is coming up. Barry's been looking forward to this for a long time; he had a great time working with him on *Big Trouble*, and he loves the guy. So the day before he's set to shoot, Johnny comes into my office. He's got crutches and his eyes are all glazed over. 'Oh my God,' I say. 'What happened?' 'I got in a motorcycle accident rehearsing for *Jackass*,' he says [referring to his highly popular MTV show, which continues to this day]. 'Barry's going to kill me.'"

/o small head

AN EARLY CONCEPT ILLUSTRATION OF JOHNNY KNOXVILLE AS CHARLIE (THE LITTLE ONE) AND SCRAD (THE BIG ONE). NOTICE THAT, FROM THE BEGINNING, CHARLIE IS A SECOND-RATE COPY OF SCRAD: BAGS UNDER THE EYES, A TWO-DAY GROWTH, LOUSY TEETH. NOT THAT ANYONE WOULD LOOK ALL THAT GREAT IF THEY LIVED IN A BACKPACK.

Kemp continued. "'You're lying,' I said. 'No,' he said, 'I did it.' He lies down on my couch, and I get a good look at him: He's got this brace on his leg, he's pale, he's even got the pills in his hand to show me. I call Barry and give him the news. He rushes to my office with Graham, and Johnny gets up. Barry says, 'Come here, let me see how bad it is.' Johnny tells him, 'I'll be able to walk tomorrow, Barry, it's okay.' He gets the crutch and starts to hobble over...and Barry screams, 'You liar, you *liar!*' So Johnny throws away the crutch and laughs, giving Barry a hug and apologizing to me. 'But...your eyes were all glazed over!' I said. He said, 'I didn't sleep last night on purpose.' 'You're pasty!' I said. 'It's powder,' he told me. He duped me...and that started a little feud between me and Johnny that lasted for the whole movie."

It wasn't actually a serious breach—how could one *not* admire that level of dedication?—but it did set the tone for working with Johnny Knoxville during the long and frequently boring days on the set.

As an actor, though, he was all that Barry Sonnenfeld could have hoped for, and more. "He'll go over the top if he has to," Sonnenfeld said. "He's ready and able to do it. But he also has the subtlety that I love."

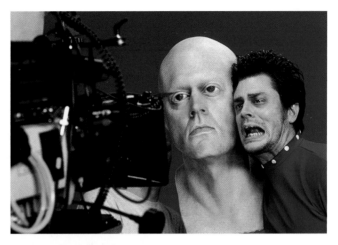

ABOVE LEFT
SCRAD EMOTES, WITH
FAKE LITTLE CHARLIE.

ABOVE
CHARLIE EMOTES, WITH
FAKE BIG SCRAD.

LEFT
THEN THE TWO SHOTS, TAKEN
MONTHS APART, HAVE TO BE
SLIPPED TOGETHER. EVERYONE
TRIES TO SEE HOW IT'S WORKING,
WITH CONSTANT HELP FROM THE
MONITORS THAT COMP THE SHOTS
TOGETHER IN REAL TIME.

"There were so many times when his performance depended on just a reaction," Kemp agreed, "or a tiny difference between Scrad and Charlie. Johnny was great. We'd be sitting at the monitor watching each take, and he'd do just a little thing a bit differently, giving Barry different options."

Still, the tedium of the technical side loomed. Early on, Knoxville had to endure a lifecast—the process of having a complete mold of his head made for the creation of a second, highly detailed false head. The cast was made at Rick Baker's Cinovation shop in Burbank, where a number of detailed reference photos were also taken.

A short time later, he'd see the result of all that tedious work: two remarkable versions of his own face and head, anatomically perfect and frighteningly lifelike. One was just inches tall—the size of Charlie as he pops out of Scrad's backpack. But the other was *huge*—scaled up to the size that Charlie would see Scrad. Knoxville would be spending a lot of time with both these heads as he began to shoot the various two-way conversations.

"We had an intricate system of puppeteers, led by Tony Urbano, who would do the second

voice, the Charlie voice, while he moved the small Charlie head in the shot, giving Scrad a sight line, a place to look," Kemp said. Then they would shoot multiple takes, as Johnny varied emphasis and timing—whatever Sonnenfeld wanted. Sonnenfeld himself and others were viewing the performance—frequently done against blue-screen, to make later compositing less difficult.

Sometime later, Sonnenfeld took the footage and put together a rough cut of that scene, including the place-marker Charlie head, and turned it over to the ILM team led by Jim Rafferty. They did their first round of comping, putting Charlie into the appropriate background.

Then came the hard part.

"Now we know, roughly, what the composition's going to be," said John Berton of ILM. "So we can go back and shoot the second part." Now Knoxville was playing the part of Charlie, the little head, and on the set he was interacting with the huge version of Scrad while listening to his own voice deliver Scrad's lines.

"When we shoot Johnny again," Berton continued, "they put him in different makeup, Charlie has bags under his eyes and a three-day beard; he's like a poor copy of Scrad." This time, they used special video and computer

ABOVE AND ABOVE RIGHT
THE REALLY REMARKABLE HEAD OF JOHNNY KNOXVILLE, MADE BY RICK BAKER STRICTLY FOR REFERENCE. UP CLOSE IT'S IMPOSSIBLE TO TELL...CHARLIE OR MEMOREX? UNTIL YOU GET A LOAD OF THAT *NECK*...

RIGHT
KNOXVILLE SPENT MOST OF HIS TIME TALKING TO SOMEONE WHO WASN'T THERE...NOT ALL THAT UNUSUAL IN LOS ANGELES.

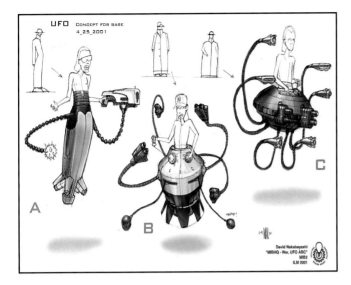

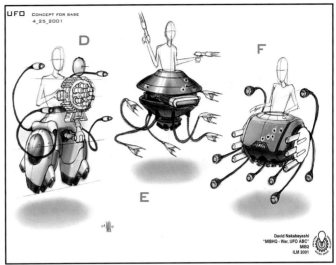

equipment to composite his performance in real time, right there on the sound set, so Knoxville could see exactly how he'd look as the small head talking to the large head. "Now we know that Charlie's in the right place, and that Scrad is looking at him. So we ship it off to ILM so they can put the shots together for the final time."

The biggest hitch was that all of this *took time*. Frequently there were monthlong gaps between Knoxville's performance as one character in the scene and his performance as the second character—it took that long for the editing and first-round composition.

Feud notwithstanding, Associate Producer Stephanie Kemp admitted that she really liked Knoxville and admired the work he did. "He was fun," she confessed. "All that blue-screen can be *so* tedious, and if you don't have someone like Johnny, who's willing to keep it interesting, it can *kill* you."

It didn't kill Johnny Knoxville. He seemed to thrive on the strange two-way character of Scrad/Charlie.

Jarra

Jarra's character began as just another one of Serleena's henchmen (henchaliens? henchentities?), but in the hands of Barry Sonnenfeld and Barry Fanaro, the concept of a Second Lieutenant Evil Genius for Serleena grew and grew in importance.

John Alexander had been tapped for the role early on, when it was still a relatively small part. Alexander—a gaunt, soft-spoken English gentleman—was one of Rick Baker's regulars, an "interesting face" whose lifecast was on file at Cinovation, and who was used frequently in various roles on Baker productions.

Jarra's appearance went through a number of iterations, all working off the same idea for the reveal...but in the final analysis he's pretty simple and pretty strange: just a large cloth cone with a head on top that floats like a ghost through MIB HQ. Then, at his final confrontation with Agent Jay, he opens his robe to show that he's actually riding in a little flying saucer of his own under that robe...and hiding half a dozen tiny versions of himself as weapons under there, as well.

> ILM WENT THROUGH A NUMBER OF VARIATIONS ON THE "JARRA AND LITTLE JARRAS" CONCEPT BEFORE SETTLING ON THE SAUCERS-WITHIN-A-SAUCER LOOK. NOTICE THAT JARRA GOT INCREASINGLY COOL (SUNGLASSES, BASEBALL CAP) AS ILM ART DIRECTOR DAVID NAKABAYASHI WENT ALONG.

ABOVE LEFT
John Alexander had worked
with Baker on many occasions,
so his lifecasts and scans
were already on file. That
made building Jarra's virtual
face on Alexander's body a
good deal easier.

ABOVE RIGHT
John Alexander as Jarra.
What began as a small Rick
Baker alien among so many oth-
ers became a major role as the
script evolved.

RIGHT
Agent Jay and Jarra share a
touching moment. Does Jarra
look in serious pain, or just
really, really bored?

The "Jarettes" would be completely computer-generated, and ILM's problem…but Costume Designer Mary Vogt worked with the *MIB* construction crew to fashion the larger Jarra's "floating rig." "It's actually a motorized wheelchair," she explained, "with a little seat on top, so he can maneuver it." A huge cowling was formed out of metal and foam rubber, to keep the black cloak he wears from fouling in the machinery, and to maintain his conical shape. The cowling would be removed by computer at ILM later, so that when Jarra whips open his robe, he's really floating in space with no visible means of support, and the nasty little Jarettes—all CG creations—would appear to be hovering inside, waiting to wreak havoc at his command.

Three great villains. All three have major digital components and practical effects…but all three *work* because of surprising and surprisingly powerful human performances.

HIGH-TECH SPECIAL EFFECTS AT THEIR FINEST. JUST SO EVERYBODY KNEW WHAT THE "JARETTES" WOULD LOOK LIKE, AND WHERE THEY WOULD BE, A SET OF THEM WAS PUT ON STICKS AND USED FOR SIGHT LINES WHEN SHOOTING.

DOSSIER

#3854

To: Manuscripts & Artifacts
From: Surveillance Team
           Gamma Delta (NYC)
Subject: The Sacred Writings of
           Interpretation (with Revealing
           Commentary)

Gaze upon the Holy Tablet of the Tapeworm, and live by its commandments. Live also by the ancient words etched in the Holy Tower of VO5: Rinse and repeat!

1. Be Kind, Rewind
Go back and reconcile your past in order to move tranquilly into the future.

2. Two for One Every Wednesday
Give twice as much as ye receive on the most sacred of days—every Wednesday.

3. Large Adult Entertainment Section in the Back
What else need be said?

Note: The reverse side of the Tablet offers words and images that require further spiritual enlightenment and deep study. Clearly the twelve Boxes of Destiny that form the Grid of Life are means to hold the Stamps of Right Action that we are meant to "collect" if we hope to "receive one (1) free rental pass"— that is, to progress to Paradise in the world beyond Lockertown.

But what is the true meaning of the words and numbers that hover above the Grid? Why is York "New"? Why does the sacred Tapeworm hide his eyes? And how can 650 be subtracted from 109?

Continue to contemplate the sacred writings. Live in peace. Contemplate the Watchtower and its descending Holy Numbers.

All will be revealed.

All Hail Kay!

(212) 109-0650
803B HUDSON ST.
NEW YORK, NY 10014

1	2	3	4	5	6
7	8	9	10	11	12

COLLECT 12 STAMPS AND RECEIVE ONE (1) FREE RENTAL PASS

BE KIND, REWIND

2 FOR 1 EVERY WEDNESDAY

LARGE **ADULT** ENTERTAINMENT
SECTION IN REAR

THE ALIENS AMONG US

CHAPTER 5

They're not like anything you'd imagine...but they're *exactly* what you expect.

The unique world of the Men in Black just wouldn't *be* that world if it weren't for the aliens, with all their specificity, physicality, and unexpected charm. There's something *real* about them; each one has a weight and substance all its own. There's the feeling that, if and when ETs ever really *do* come to Earth, they're going to look like one of the creatures from the *MIB* movies. They strike that kind of genuine chord.

One reason the aliens work so well for audiences around the world is their hidden consistency. They're not clichéd or predictable, but they *are* of a piece—the product of a consistent point of view. That viewpoint itself is a gestalt of Barry Sonnenfeld, Rick Baker, and Bo Welch, with contributions from a wide variety of artists and designers.

Bo Welch, as Production Designer, created the environment in which the creatures dwell, and provided a welcome and essential third set of eyes as the creatures were developed. But the primary collaboration, alienwise, was between Sonnenfeld and Baker.

"Barry and Rick have a great relationship," observed Stephanie Kemp. "They tease, they argue, they push each other constantly...but they respect each other. They enjoy their work together."

Sonnenfeld had the vision—an absolutely clear idea in his head of what each alien was supposed to do and what it was supposed to accomplish. Baker was an inexhaustible wellspring of new ideas, inspirations, and imagery. What they produced together possessed a unique energy—different from anything each of these two talented individuals might do independently.

"The early meetings were very interesting," one staffer recalled. "It would be Barry and Graham Place, Bo Welch, Stephanie Kemp, Stunt Coordinator Charlie Croughwell, sometimes Walter Parkes and Laurie MacDonald...and Rick and his guys would put up boards, and show us literally the creatures we'd use in the movie. We were all simply mesmerized, asking ourselves, *Who comes up with this stuff?* And Barry—in addition to being mesmerized—is being absolutely specific about what he wants these creatures to be. 'That one has to have long

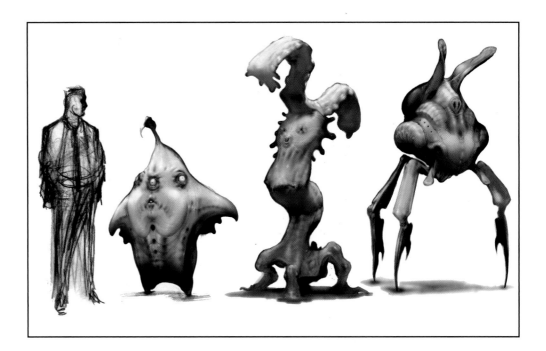

tentacles. *That* one has to be cuter. That one has to be meaner. That one has to be purple.' Unless you have a mind like that, unless you are so specific about what you want, it would be impossible to go into Rick Baker's and *not* just gasp and say, *Yes yes yes yes yes, put it* all *in.*"

"I don't read science fiction, or go to sci-fi movies," Sonnenfeld said. "I've never seen *The Shining* or *Carrie* or anything like that. They're simply too frightening for me. And sometimes that can get in the way when we're making these aliens—I'm not always sure what's been done and what hasn't. We spent all that time working on Edgar Bug in the first movie—all that energy trying to make him really work—and then when it finally comes out, I hear a kid in a test screening say, 'Oh, it looks just like *Predator.*'" He sighed at that. "Great."

Actually, Sonnenfeld's lack of familiarity with every new bugaboo to hit the screen has proved to be a *good* thing—it's been one of the reasons his own vision has remained fresh and unexpected. It's *not* cluttered with references and homages and leftovers from other people's pictures.

What's equally important is that over time, Sonnenfeld and Baker have developed a vocabulary of their own—not as extensive or explicit as Welch's architectural language, but a set of rules that still apply consistently across the board.

RULE ONE: KEEP IT CONNECTED. Whether the alien has skin like an alligator, eyes like a cat, a mouth like your Aunt Hildy's, or jowls that dangle like human genitalia, it has to possess *some* characteristic that's familiar to the casual viewer—some connection to real life. "There has to be a familiar quality to the creature," Sonnenfeld said, "or it just doesn't work—you don't believe it."

RULE TWO: SIZE DOESN'T MATTER. The aliens can be so small that a fingertip can send a tidal wave across their entire landscape, as with the poor Jarithians, who get fingered by a predeneuralyzed Kay, or so huge that they can swallow a subway car without even breaking a sweat.

RULE THREE: RESPECT THE UNEXPECTED. The best aliens are the ones that *don't* act as you expect them to: a perfectly normal pug dog…who suddenly tells you to kiss his furry butt. A huge

LEFT
MOSH BULB IN CONCEPT,
ENJOYING A DRINK—ONE OF MANY
ALIENS FOR THE "STRIP MALL"
SEQUENCE. ART BY
CARLOS HUANTE

FAR LEFT
RICK BAKER'S CREW CREATES A
HIGHLY DETAILED SCULPTURE FOR
APPROVAL—THE KEY REFERENCE
FOR ALL THAT COMES AFTER.

BELOW
CHRIS AYERS OF CINOVATION
AIRBRUSHES A LATEX SUIT MOLD
FOR A MEMBER OF THE
VOMIT FAMILY.

worm who looks absolutely goofy, more Cecil the Sea Serpent than Sauron...until he opens his mouth to show row after row of vicious teeth. A human head that pops open to reveal a "driver" no bigger than a hamster.

RULE FOUR: DON'T WORRY ABOUT "HOW," WORRY ABOUT "HOW FUNNY." "I don't really understand a lot of this special-effects technology," Sonnenfeld revealed, maybe with more than a little false modesty. "But I know that Rick Baker or John Berton or *somebody* can make almost any idea work. My job is to come up with good ideas. I let people who are much smarter than I am make those ideas real."

Some aliens are really rubber suits; some are purely digital. Most are a cunning combination of technologies that run the gamut from puppetry to stop-action animation...and *none of this matters* to Sonnenfeld. What matters is that they look right, and that they're part of some larger gag, some more extravagant piece of action that's going to move the story forward and make the audience laugh...or preferably *both*.

RIGHT
JEREMY HOWARD WAS ANOTHER LONGTIME BAKER ASSOCIATE, WITH HUNDREDS OF SCANS AND LIFE-CASTS ON FILE. "I HAD BEEN THINKING ABOUT A BIRD ALIEN SINCE WE USED HIM ON *GRINCH*," BAKER SAID. *MEN IN BLACK II* PROVIDED HIS CHANCE TO MAKE THAT HAPPEN.

FAR RIGHT
THE FULL-HEAD SCULPTURE WAS MADE FROM BAKER'S HIGHLY DETAILED RENDERING.

MID RIGHT
HIS YELLOW-HAIRED PARTNER GOT THE SAME EXACTING ATTENTION FROM MITCH DEVANE—SCULPTING HERE ON A BUST OF ACTRESS MARY STEIN. NOTICE THE GRIDS ON THE GLASSES, HELPING THE MASK MAKER TO DUPLICATE THE FORM TO SCALE.

BELOW
THE REDHEADED BIRD IN FULL FEATHER.

BELOW RIGHT
THE BIRDS ON THE SET. NOTHIN' TO IT.

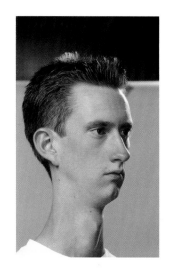

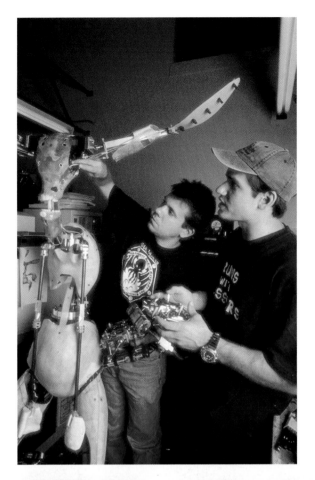

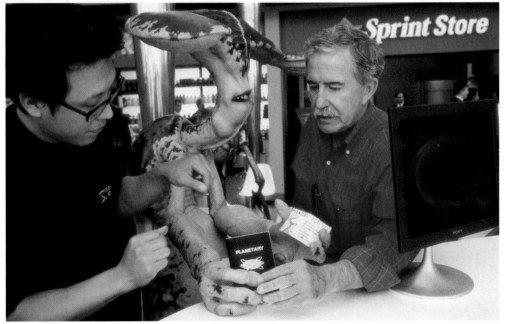

ABOVE LEFT
THE SAME PROCESS USED
IN CREATING THE "ORGANIC"
EXTRATERRESTRIALS WAS APPLIED
BY PETER ABRAMSON (LEFT) AND
KYLE MARTIN (RIGHT) TO THE
PURELY MECHANICAL ALIENS
SCULPTURE...

ABOVE
...**F**ULLY PAINTED
FOR REFERENCE...

LEFT
THEN DESIGNER/SCULPTOR
EDDIE YOUNG (LEFT) AND
PUPPETEER TONY URBANO (RIGHT)
BUILT THE CHARACTER TO SIZE, WITH
ALL THE MACHINERY IN PLACE.

TOP
THE MOST CHALLENGING
CREATURES WERE A COMBINATION
OF MASK AND ROBOTICS.
LIKE THE SHARK GUY,
WHO BEGAN AS A MASK...

BOTTOM RIGHT
...THEN THE MACHINERY WAS ADDED
BY MECHANIC/PUPPETEER
BUD MCGREW...

ABOVE
...UNTIL THE FINAL DETAILING
WAS COMPLETE...

TOP RIGHT
...AND HE APPEARED ON THE SET,
COSTUMED AND READY TO ROAR.

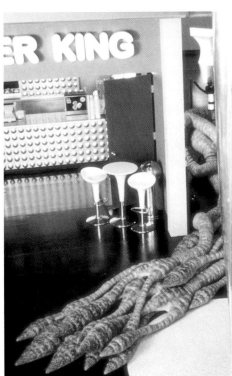

LEFT
ALL THE EFFORT PROVES WORTHWHILE WHEN THE RESULT IS A CONVINCING, IMPORTANT—AND WEIRD—AUTOPSY ALIEN.

BELOW
EVEN THE NONMOVING CREATURES GOT THE FULL TREATMENT FROM CINOVATION'S BART MIXON, SUPERVISOR OF THE AUTOPSY ALIEN. MOLDS WERE MADE, LATEX POURED, PIECES GLUED TOGETHER AND PAINTED. FOR DAYS AND DAYS AND DAYS.

BELOW LEFT
THE REFERENCE PHOTO TRAVELED WITH THE CREATURE THROUGHOUT THE PROCESS, RIGHT UP TO ITS ARRIVAL ON THE SET.

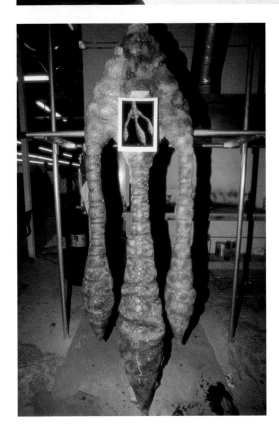

RIGHT
SOME "LOOKS" SHOW MORE OF THE ORIGINAL FACE THAN OTHERS, AS WITH THE THIRD EYE GUY, KEVIN GREVIOUX, WHO BEGAN AS A SCULPTURE OVER A CAST OF GREVIOUX'S FACE.

FAR RIGHT
APPLIANCES WERE BUILT TO COVER GREVIOUX'S OWN HAIR AND GIVE HIM THAT CHARMING ADDITIONAL ORB.

BOTTOM
BIGGER EARS AND TOTAL MAKEUP BLEND THE LOOK ALL TOGETHER...

...AND THE HAIRPIECE JUST MAKES IT SING.

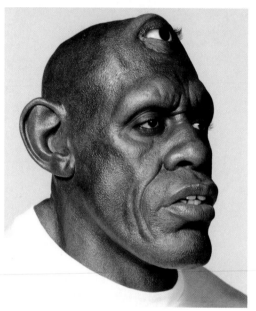

These rules of the road, along with half a dozen others that remain unarticulated, combine to create a very definite, very specific *look and feel* for the aliens in *Men in Black*. And once that look and feel was established, what remained was for the creative team to wrestle over whether it would be ILM's job or Rick's or Charlie's or *whose* to make that creature get up and walk around.

Rick Baker was clearly the point man in this process. Not only had he produced more monsters than anyone else working today, but he *got* it, too. Time after time, Sonnenfeld would approve Baker's first sketch or rendering with a quick yes, and they moved on to the next issue. Other designers, other artists, quickly found that they had to please Baker as much as Sonnenfeld...and that wasn't necessarily an easy thing to do.

As for the technologies...rubber mask? Computerized creature? A puppet, a contortionist, a

little person, a radio-controlled robot? The aliens of *MIB II* were all that and more—and frequently they were the focal point where a combination of techniques and technologies came together. Regardless, though, the technologies were all a means to an end—and the end was to make a brand-new creature that the audience would *believe* in.

ABOVE AND RIGHT
DESPITE THE COMPLEX PROCESS, AN AMAZING AMOUNT OF THE LOOK AND FEEL OF THE ALIENS REMAINED CONSTANT, FROM RENDERING TO FINAL FORM....AS WITH ROBOSQUID.

BELOW
AN EARLY DESIGN FOR A BAD GUY WHO DIDN'T MAKE IT INTO THE FILM.

BELOW RIGHT
AN EARLY BIRD GUY DESIGN BY KAZUHIRO TSUJI (LEFT), A MAILROOM ALIEN DESIGNED BY CHET ZAR (RIGHT).

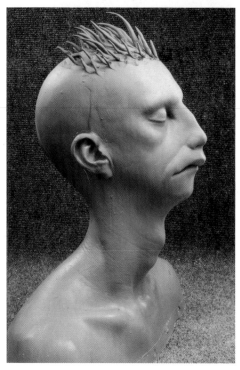

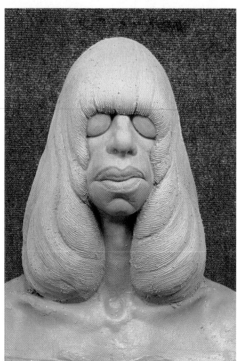

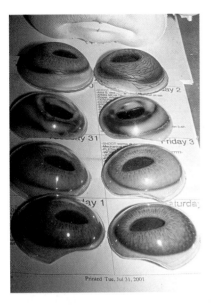

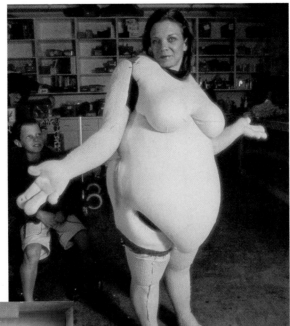

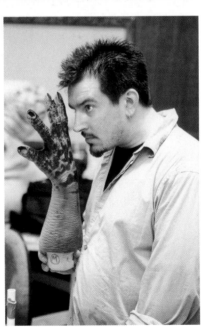

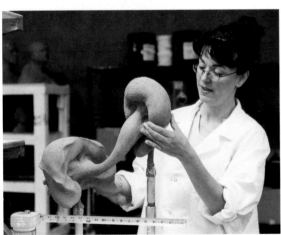

BELOW LEFT
None of it happens without the artisans behind the scenes. Here, Beate Eisele works on a sculpture.

CENTER
Joe Gomez, Cory Czekaj, and Frank Rydberg work on the mold for "Pretzel Guy," who didn't even appear in the film.

BELOW RIGHT
It *can* get a little intense at times. Mark Jurinko gives himself a hand.

ABOVE RIGHT
It's all in the details. Here: a selection of eyes for the Lockertown Aliens.

ABOVE RIGHT
Denise Cheshire models an alien suit without the skin and makeup. The appliances on the legs and the arm extension help to disguise normal human body proportions as much as possible.

Printed Tue, Jul 31, 2001

The GatBot, also called Little Killing Robot, shoots at anything that moves during the final retaking of MIB HQ, and he was the result of a long series of development projects. "At first, Barry wanted him to look like a lipstick case," said John Berton. "Then one of the drawings looked like a trash can. So the director looked at the production designer, and they said, 'Hey, make it a trash can.'" Thus was GatBot born. Art by James Carson

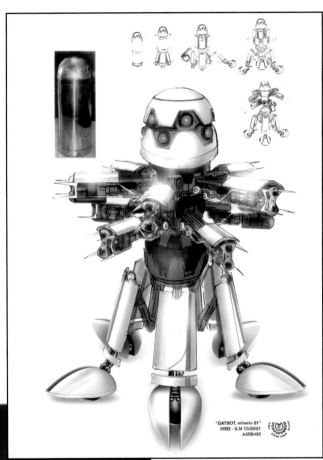

"GATBOT, wheels 01"
MIB2 - ILM 10/09/01
AMIB488

ART BY DAVID NAKABAYASHI (ABOVE) AND
JAMES CARSON (LEFT)

DOSSIER

To: Zed
From: Cliff's Clipping Service
Subject: Unauthorized "Deneuralyzer"
          Manual Field Operation

HEY, KIDS! MAKE YOUR OWN DENEURALYZER AT HOME!

Have you been neuralyzed? How would you know? Here's your chance to send trans-verse magneto energy surging through your brain, unlocking information hidden deep and dormant. You might save the world! Or maybe you'll just find those car keys you lost last summer.

Just follow these simple schematics, and you're on your way!

Note: Micro-encapsulated transverse energy cold fusion condenser not included. Contact your local MIB office for authorization.

1 Truck Tire

2 Sunlamps

3 Bowling Ball

4 Stovepipe

5 Barcalounger
   (Hydromassage may be substituted)

6 Stepladder

7 Head Clamp

8 Leg Braces
   (skateboards may be substituted)

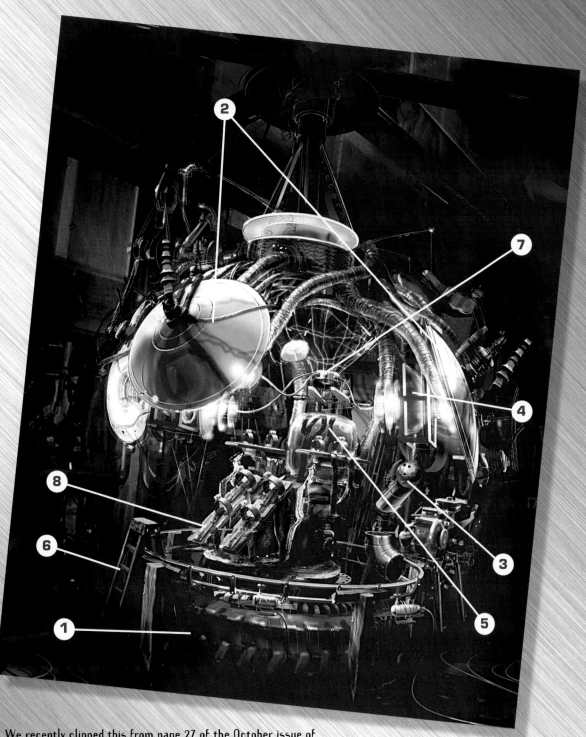

We recently clipped this from page 27 of the October issue of
Wowzers! Popular Engineering for Kids!, a monthly throwaway for elementary school children. Is this of any interest to
you?

CHAPTER 6

WHEELS, WINGS, WIDGETS, AND WEAPONS

Past the architecture, beyond the aliens, in addition to the actors and the digital effects, there's another thing that makes *Men in Black* something special:

Cool junk.

Bo Welch's extraordinary attention to detail has led directly to the invention of half a hundred different gadgets—from alien detectors to spaceships, from the neuralyzer to rocket-shoes—all of which fit comfortably into the world of MIB.

How does he do it? It's like the low-priced used-car sales-man: *volume.*

"We just crank it out," Welch revealed. "No matter what, though, you end up designing much more than you need."

The concept-illustration stage is smoother and more exten-sive than it used to be, thanks to the computers and an extraor-dinarily talented group of designers and illustrators. Building the creations falls to the prop people, and they've proven to be geniuses at fabrication on a short schedule. "Most often we make molds," Welch said. "But sometimes [the props will be] kludged together from found objects."

Not that it's always easy...or that the props always work. The neuralyzer, for instance—a device that's central to the plot of both movies, and a key to understanding how the MIB works —was "an unwieldy prop," according to Tommy Lee Jones. A wonderful concept, yes, but the device proved unfor-tunately unable to both open up and flash in the same take. "I thought that wouldn't be a problem," Sonnenfeld admitted. "I told Doug Harlocker, 'Don't worry, we won't need it to do both things in the same take.' And of course...we always did."

Whenever there's a hinge to open, a display to light up, or a switch to flip, there's the potential for malfunction...which is why there's a remarkable absence of "working props" in *MIB II.* Almost all the sounds, actions, and light effects were added digitally by Industrial Light & Magic, long after principal photography had ended, just as all the rods, wires, cables, and harnesses were carefully removed from each and every appro-priate frame. In the world of modern moviemaking, at least, *form* is far more important than *function.* In fact, form will beat the crap out of function every time.

The eventual use of the tool or weapon dictated just how sturdy it had to be, and how much attention to detail had to

RIGHT AND BELOW
THE COOLEST GADGET YOU
NEVER SAW: WILL SMITH'S
ROCKET-SHOES, GIVEN THE
SOMEHOW INEVITABLE NAME OF
"BALL THRUSTERS."

RIGHT MIDDLE
THE ALIEN IDENTIFIER, EVIDENT
IN THE TRURO POST OFFICE
SCENE AND ELSEWHERE.

BOTTOM RIGHT
DANG, EVEN THE *KEY CHAINS* ARE
COOL. JAMES CARSON
EXECUTED THIS EXTRAORDINARY
PIECE OF WORK.

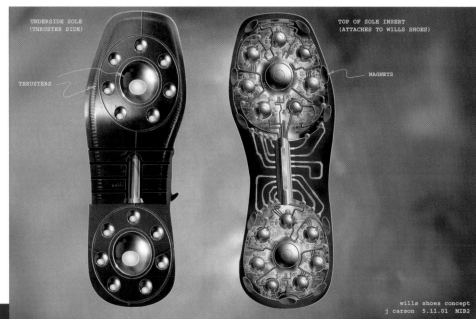

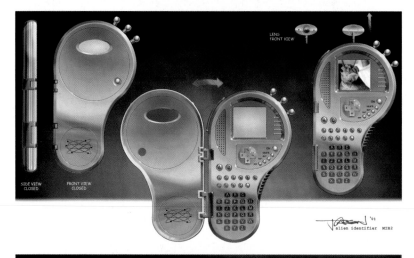

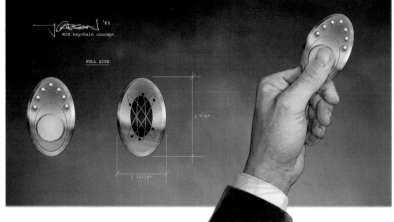

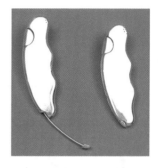

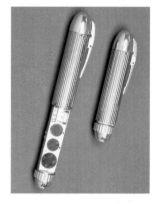

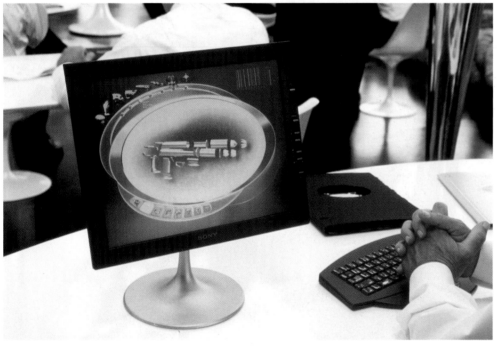

TOP
THE COMMUNICATORS, WITHOUT A
DOUBT THE COOLEST CELL PHONES
EVER DESIGNED.

ABOVE
THE "UNWIELDY" NEURALYZERS,
AT REST AND AT WORK. THOUGH
THEY'VE GAINED SOME DETAIL IN
THE LAST FOUR YEARS, THEY CON-
TINUE TO LOOK LIKE THE WORLD'S
MOST DANGEROUS FOUNTAIN PEN

LEFT
A STANDARD MIB COMPUTER
WORKSTATION, DESIGNED MONTHS
BEFORE THE NEW FLAT-SCREEN
IMACS WERE REVEALED.
COINCIDENCE...OR SOMETHING
MORE?

ABOVE LEFT
EVEN THE AUTOPSY TOOLS
NEEDED TO BE DESIGNED AND
BUILT SPECIALLY FOR THE FILM.
AUDIENCES GET A GLIMPSE OF
THEM AS THE BIG DEAD ALIEN
PASSES BY AGAIN AND AGAIN
AND *AGAIN*.

be applied. The weapons in Kay's old apartment were a good example. "In that case," Welch said, "we went to the toy store and bought giant water guns and painted them. The guns were only going to be in the background, and seen from a distance, so mostly they're just water guns from Toys "R" Us. But as you get closer, they become more and more important...so we added a couple of more complete models for Will and Tommy to actually pick up, check out, put down. You have to prioritize things like that.

FRANCOIS AUDOUY'S FINAL RENDERINGS OF THE MIB HAZMAT VEHICLE, TRUCK OF CHOICE FOR ALL DISCERNING MIB ALIEN CLEANUP TEAM MEMBERS.

HAZMAT TRANSPORT VEHICLE

ELEVATION

ELEVATION - SIDE VIEW

AUDOUY
MIB HAZMAT TROOP TRANSPORT
MEN IN BLACK II

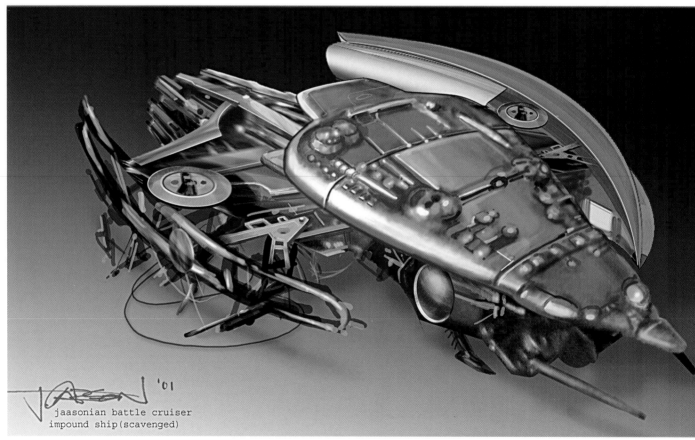

jaasonian battle cruiser
impound ship (scavenged)

'01

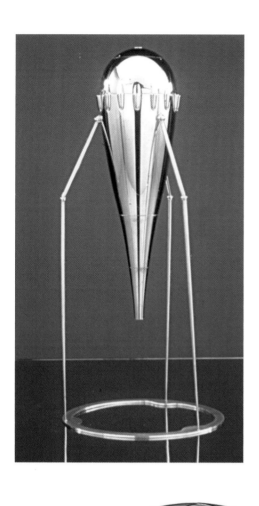

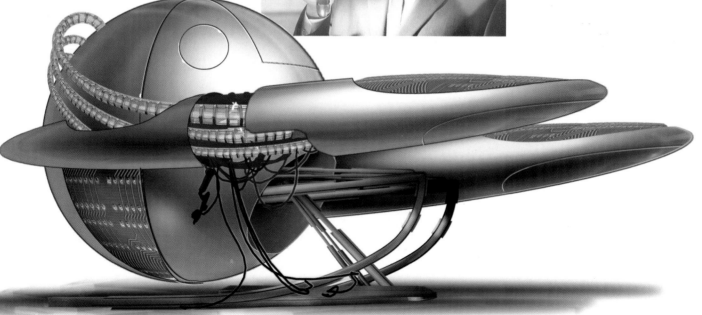

ABOVE
EVEN THE INSIDE OF
SERLEENA'S SHIP WAS COMPLETED
IN MINUTE DETAIL, ON THE
CHANCE THAT SOME TAKES
WOULD INCLUDE A CLEAR VIEW
OF THE CONSOLE.

TOP
THE "ROCK SHIP" THAT TAKES
THE LIGHT BACK TO ZARTHA WENT
THROUGH A NUMBER OF ITERATIONS;
THIS SHINY CHROME EGG WAS ONE
OF MANY.

ABOVE AND RIGHT
3D MODEL MAKER
PAUL OZZIMO TOOK BO WELCH'S
ORIGINAL SKETCHES FOR
SERLEENA'S CHASE-AND-DESTROY
SHIP, THEN PRODUCED THIS
STUNNING MODEL FOR THE CON-
STRUCTION CREW. A FEW TONS OF
SHEET STEEL AND PLASTIC
LATER...AND *VOILÀ*.

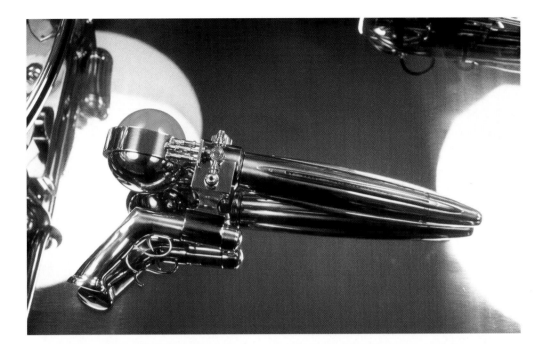

A TRUNKFUL OF CREATURE-CRUSHING, MONSTER-MASHING MAYHEM. DON'T LEAVE HOME WITHOUT 'EM.

RIGHT
One of James Carson's designs for a sleek chrome hand grenade.

CENTER
This rifle-sized version of Agent Jay's Noisy Cricket looked "cute" to Bo Welch.

BELOW
The major-league bazooka never made the final cut, but it is beautiful in an evil, incendiary sort of way.
All art this page by James Carson

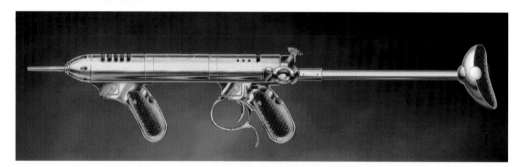

MELEE
BREAK IN EMERGENCY

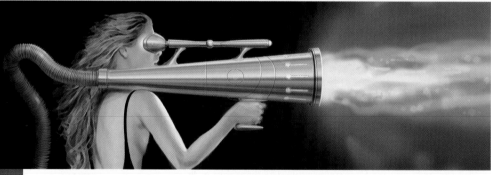

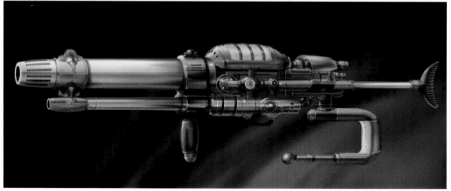

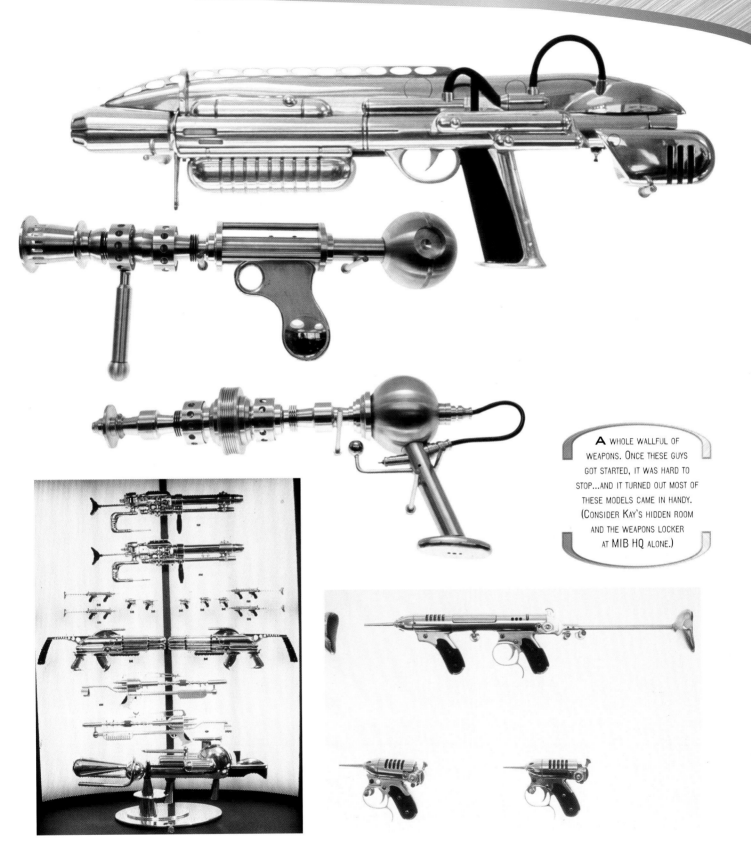

A WHOLE WALLFUL OF
WEAPONS. ONCE THESE GUYS
GOT STARTED, IT WAS HARD TO
STOP...AND IT TURNED OUT MOST OF
THESE MODELS CAME IN HANDY.
(CONSIDER KAY'S HIDDEN ROOM
AND THE WEAPONS LOCKER
AT MIB HQ ALONE.)

RIGHT
THE PROTON DETONATOR.
HOW CAN SOMETHING LOOK SO
BEAUTIFUL AND BE SO EVIL AT
THE SAME TIME? OTHER THAN
SERLEENA, THAT IS.

BOTTOM RIGHT
THE PROTON DETONATOR IN
"REAL LIFE," LOOKING MORE
LIKE A RELIGIOUS ARTIFACT
THAN A DEVASTATING BOMB.
ART BY JAMES CARSON

pre-activated stage

KEVIN
BROWN

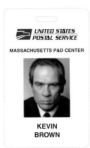

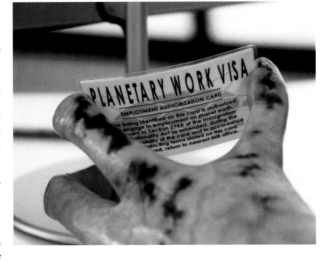

"If it's in the script, I'll design it," Welch added...but since the script was in a continual state of revision, that resulted in a fair number of wonderful designs that never got past the development stage. These included a marvelous set of rocket-shoes for Will Smith called "ball thrusters" that could make somebody a fortune if they ever actually *existed*.

Whether it was built or languished on the conceptual artist's board, everything in the world of the Men in Black had to be *designed*. Nothing was left to chance; nothing could simply be picked up from the local prop house or pulled in from the street. Bo Welch set himself an awesome goal when he created these two self-contained worlds, and in turn, he and his crew found themselves designing everything from trash cans to immigration documents, in ways that became both convincing and clever. Some will be recognized; others won't, and many will never be seen again. But they're all part of the larger picture. They're all *MIB*.

IF JAY'S GOING TO BE RIDING WORMS IN THE SUBWAY TUNNELS, HE'S GOING TO NEED AN MTA CARD, ISN'T HE? NOTE: IT'S GOOD UNTIL 2013.

ABOVE LEFT
THE TRUTH IS FINALLY KNOWN. AGENT J = JAMES EDWARDS; AGENT K = KEVIN BROWN. HMM..."JAY" AND "KAY" SOUND MUCH COOLER.

ABOVE
SERLEENA'S PLANETARY PASSPORT AND WORK VISA, OBVIOUSLY A FORGERY—*HER* PICTURE LOOKS GOOD. (IT ALSO LISTS HER LAST NAME AS "LACE" INSTEAD OF "XATH" AND GIVES HER BIRTH PLANET AS "VENUS," WHEN *EVERYBODY* KNOWS SHE WAS BORN ON JORN. HOW STUPID DO THEY THINK WE *ARE*?)

LEFT
A LEGITIMATE PLANETARY WORK VISA, IN THE HANDS OF A GOOD, HARDWORKING ALIEN ON EARTH. HOW CAN YOU TELL HE'S HARDWORKING? IT'S OBVIOUS: HE'S ALREADY WORKED HIS FINGERS TO THE BONE...

#1222

To: Chief Disinformant 6
          Department of Data Manipulation
          MIB Office 2-391-3
From: Submanipulator B
Subject: Damage Control: Media Leak
          (television)

MYSTERIES IN HISTORY: "SECRETS REVEALED!"

You must have seen this show. Didn't
you? Big hit in syndication back in
the 1970s. And it used to be on
TVLand, just before the infomercials
at 3 A.M.

Okay, never mind. In fact,
Mysteries in History is entirely made
up—a mythical low-rent version of a
thousand other "real," and the term
is used *very* loosely in this context,
TV series about the unex-

plained, the unknown, the unexpected.

Though on screen we see only a few
short seconds of this truly awful
program, it's an all-important stimu-
lus to Kay's memory of the Light of
Zartha—a major plot point in *Men in
Black II*. It was also one of the
favorite mini-projects of the *MIB*
crew.

The Art Department got into the act
by creating a whole series of
Mysteries in History videotapes—a
bookshelf full of 'em, for Newton to
paw through while looking for the
Light of Zartha. The box used garish
1970s typefaces and design, and even
featured a contemporary picture of
Peter Graves, circa his *Mission:
Impossible* days.

Since the sequence itself, including both the bad re-creation and the
"real" flashback, would take up only
a few seconds of screen time, there
was no chance that the crew would be
flying to a cornfield somewhere in
the Midwest to shoot it. Instead, the
location scout found a field in Van
Nuys—in the San Fernando Valley, not

Forget those Smith and Jones guys. This here is a
real celebrity, and even the jaded been-there-
done-that-seen-it-all-before-lunch cast and crew
were impressed with his one-day shoot. "He is
just cool," Stephanie Kemp said. "Just *so cool*."
Mysteries in History's black-and-white vision of
the MIB, complete with high-tech weaponry and
space-age cars.

far from the Sony Pictures Entertainment Studios in Culver City— where the MIB could grow its own corn. That's right: *grow its own corn.*

"It was *huge*," Stephanie Kemp said. "The tallest corn any of us had ever seen. Barry was so shocked when he saw it, he asked, 'Why'd we go all the way to Santa Fe for *Wild Wild West?*'—we could have done it right here in the valley."

All the pros had a field day doing

The "real" Lauranna isn't a corn-fed beauty queen...but can anyone blame Kay for falling in love with her? A glimpse of a slightly soaked but much younger Agent Kay.

some of their very worst work for the re-creation shoot. It was a festival of beat-up vintage cars, bad suits, bad hair, and aliens with heads that looked like lightbulbs.

"It was ninety-five degrees on the day of the shoot," Stephanie Kemp said. "And here was Paige Brooks, fake Princess Lauranna—she was Miss Alabama 1998, you know, she was the real deal—tromping around in the field in six-inch platforms and a metallic micromini, along with these aliens with these big fishbowl heads, sweating in their foil outfits. Since it's the Seventies, the Men in Black have Afros, wide lapels, a Pacer, and Ray·Ban Aviators."

Though it was officially a second-unit project, Barry Sonnenfeld decided to show up. He was slated to direct the flashback sequence that night on the same location...and he couldn't resist seeing just how bad *Mysteries* was really going to be.

"He was funny," Kemp said. "He said, 'Why can't it be this fun all

DOSSIER

The "real" meeting between the Zarthan and the Kylothians, with MIB in the middle.
Serleena, her teeny spaceship, her horn-o'-plenty ray gun, and corn grown especially for *MIB II*.

the time?' I mean, it's hot out there in the cornfield, and the beauty queen stumbling through the dirt, bringing this Light of Zartha thing to the Men in Black, and Barry says, 'Maybe it should be in a box—does anybody have a box?' We're sitting here shooting this thing, making it up as we go along. And of course Doug Harlocker, our prop master, says, 'I have several boxes; what kind would you like?' He comes up with ten different, absolutely *beautiful* boxes, and Barry says, 'I don't know...*that* one.' It was the most relaxed day of the entire shoot."

That night, *MIB II*'s first unit came in and used exactly the same setup in the cornfield to shoot the "true" flashback, with entirely different actors. But this time they lit it properly, brought in the accurate MIB costumes circa 1975 or so, and featured Serleena's real spaceship in

the background. They even rolled in huge rain machines and dumped thousands of gallons of water on everyone—a classic Midwest storm. Even so—the same cornfield, the same clearing—the parallels lend an eerie credibility to both scenes, though those *Mysteries* people got it *all* wrong.

"They shot it in the daytime—it was night. They had it sunny—it was raining. And even though the real Princess Lauranna was beautiful, she's a tiny little woman, not a former Miss Alabama."

But as much fun as the day in the cornfield was for everyone, the real thrill was meeting Peter Graves. "He was so hilarious," Stephanie said, "because he is so serious, and so regal—absolutely straight—but on the cheesiest set you've ever seen. It's as if Peter Graves lost his A&E deal and ran out of money gambling, and had no choice but to take this show. So he sits at his crappy little desk with this terrible painting in the back, in front of a wall of fake books, and then he swivels to one side and this sad wall opens up to become a [star] field. It was *awful*...and he was *great*."

It was only a one-day shoot, but cast and crew alike were fascinated. "It was Peter Graves. We were all a little starstruck."

Francois Audouy's vision of the silo opening to reveal the ship, and the classic *It Came from Outer Space* vehicle hiding inside.

CHAPTER 7

HALF A DOZEN SPECIAL-EFFECTS SANDWICHES TO GO (FAST!)

Making It Happen

Like any successful action picture, *Men in Black II* offered a dizzying series of fight scenes and chase scenes. As much as the wonderful characters and vivid effects, those fight and chase scenes are essential to the finished film…and there are three Hollywood Truths that apply to the process of making them happen:

1. Planning, right down to the tiniest detail, is absolutely essential.

2. The scene will take twice as long as you expected, even if you've doubled your original estimate.

3. The shoot often will be incredibly, *incredibly* b-o-r-i-n-g.

All three rules applied, to one degree or another, to the key action sequences in *Men in Black II,* even before the arduous work with Industrial Light & Magic began in earnest.

This particular film was distinguished by its heavy use of "practical effects"—full-sized explosions, wind effects, real water in real tanks, actual people in real live rubber suits. There was virtually no work in miniatures, and most of the pyrotechnics and even light effects were done on stage, in real time. Consequently, planning and setup often took longer; there were so many more details, and so many things that could go wrong.

A few key scenes, as they were shot, showed some of the extraordinary challenges the cast and crew faced.

Serleena Conquers the MIB

One woman in lingerie, a two-headed guy with a knapsack, and MIB HQ falls in a matter of moments. What's this world coming to? Blame it on the element of surprise, and on the Kylothian neural roots, but it certainly happened *fast.*

At least it happened fast in the *movie.*

On the set, the "attack" sequence took days to shoot…even though some of the "neural root" segment was left for later.

At the outset, the Art Department supplied drawings of a variety of MIB personnel, trapped by Serleena's diabolical roots. They were hurled about, and slammed up against the glass walls of some of the HQ alcoves. For some productions, all that complex work would be executed in a computer later. But for *Men in Black II,* the creative team resolved to have many of those elements built right into the set. Ultimately, viewers will catch glimpses of six sculpted MIB agents trapped in three rooms, their bodies held at bizarre angles and tangled in a mass of gnarled neural roots. The rest of the action took place right there on stage, with the filmmakers constantly referring to storyboards that showed Serleena shooting miles and *miles* of roots into the air, filling the entire place. The combination of the vivid illustrations and the bodies trapped in the brambles was enough to give everyone the jitters.

LEFT AND BELOW

FRANCOIS AUDOUY'S RENDERINGS OF MEN IN BLACK, TRAPPED IN THE ROOTS, ARE ACTUALLY PRETTY CREEPY; THE FULL-SIZED, REAL-LIFE RENDITIONS THAT APPEARED ON THE SETS ARE EVEN CREEPIER.

BOTTOM

HOLLYWOOD RULE ONE: PLAN RIGHT DOWN TO THE LAST DETAIL. THAT'S WHY EVERY SEQUENCE— LIKE THE GATBOT'S RAMPAGE THROUGH HEADQUARTERS—WAS STORYBOARDED SHOT FOR SHOT, AND THE STORYBOARDS THEMSELVES WERE KEPT ON THE SET FOR CON- STANT REFERENCE.

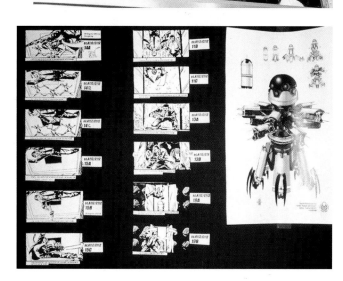

TOP
THE DEPRESSURIZATION
SEQUENCE MAY HAVE BEEN THE
SINGLE MESSIEST SET OF TAKES
THAT THE CREW HAD TO ENDURE.
NO WONDER THEY WRAPPED THEM-
SELVES IN PLASTIC TO KEEP THE
GUNK OFF.

MIDDLE RIGHT
MMMM. MOVIEMAKING IS
SO...APPETIZING.

MIDDLE LEFT
CUE THE STUNTMEN. CUE THE AIR
CANNON. CUE THE SNACK FOOD.
RELEASE THE DOGS!

BOTTOM
INCOMING! TUCK AND ROLL,
TUCK AND ROLL!

Depressurization, Ho!

When Bo Welch first designed the MIB entrance alcove for the elevator scene, he didn't think for a minute that it might be the site of a major windstorm only a few years later. But there it is: massive depressurization as Jay and Kay blast their way into the locked-down, overtaken MIB HQ.

Making the explosive decompression look realistic proved to be a massive job, involving, among other things, huge fans and shovels full of hot dogs and buns (the wind upset a hot dog vendor just outside the door, y'see).

The final scene involved two stuntmen rolling on the ground, while pressurized air was shot from cannons, and two grown men stood there flinging lunch meat. There was so much debris in the air that the camera crew fashioned protective gear out of plastic wrap.

The Truro Post Office Goes All Alien

Certainly one of the most complicated and time-consuming setups in the movie, the Truro Post Office scene had to be shot twice: once with the actors in "normal" attire, doing their best to look perfectly natural; then a second time, when virtually all the workers—in the same places, in the same outfits—revealed themselves to be the aliens they truly are.

POST OFFICE Sc. 45
Split guy
PRE-reveal
Straight makeup

Need actor
-Need to discuss straight makeup and hair.

POST OFFICE Sc. 45
Split guy
POST-reveal
Animatronic puppet

Need actor
-Seen in 2 shot after reveal with Eye guy. Need pit in floor to hide lower half of actor.

POST OFFICE Sc. 45
EyeGuy
PRE-reveal
Straight makeup

Barry Shabaka Henley?
-Need to discuss straight makeup and hair.

POST OFFICE Sc. 45
EyeGuy
POST-reveal
Animatronic puppet

Barry Shabaka Henley?
-Seen in 2 shot with split guy.

ABOVE
MORE PLANNING. THESE RELATIVELY SIMPLE BEFORE-AND-AFTER PHOTOSHOP IMAGES GIVE EVERYONE A STRONG VISUAL SENSE OF WHAT THE EFFECTS WILL LOOK LIKE AND HOW THEY'LL BE ACHIEVED—USING STRAIGHT MAKEUP, ANIMATRONICS, AND WHATEVER ELSE IS NEEDED.

BELOW LEFT
THE POST OFFICE IN MIDTRANS-FORMATION. "SPLIT GUY," IN THE MIDDLE OF THE FLOOR, IS NONE OTHER THAN ILM VISUAL EFFECTS SUPERVISOR JOHN BERTON.

BELOW
EYE GUY WITH HIS HEAD IN HIS HANDS—LITERALLY.

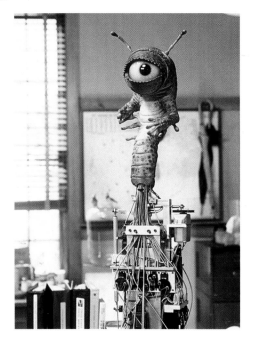

Character makeup, full masks, prosthetics, stage magic, computer graphics, and the kitchen sink were used to make this scene work, in a Rick Baker extravaganza that brought a whole new meaning to the term *going postal*.

Bring Me the Skin of Ben of Soho

Alas, poor Ben. Audiences barely get to meet him before Serleena lifts him off the ground by the neck, and slits the human skin right off his Zarthan body. But they *do* get a pretty good look at the skin itself, lying on the chipped linoleum of the pizzeria.

It's so realistic that no one would guess that this intricate and detailed suit *didn't* belong to Jack Kehler, the actor who played Ben. In fact, it was the same latex lifecast that Rick Baker made for Vincent D'Onofrio as Edgar in *Men in Black.* A quick change to the hairline, add the right clothes, and *bang,* poor Ben is dead.

Sometimes it's actually *easier* than it looks.

The Rumble in the Tunnel

As if Jeebs's basement wasn't cluttered enough...imagine the mess after a host of ugly thugs smashed through the wall and started a massive fistfight. This showcase for some of Baker's best aliens also involved some serious pyrotechnics (in blowing down the wall), complicated fight choreography, and one of the strangest rigs Charlie Croughwell and Tom Fisher made for the film.

The alien commonly known as Cornface was called upon to lift Agent Jay off the ground, hold him over his head, and bend him like a pretzel. Sonnenfeld wanted as much as possible of this effect to be in real time; he wanted it close-up and gritty, and that meant actually hanging Will Smith from the ceiling, so that Cornface could bend him all he wanted.

Still, the problem: How to get the angle Sonnenfeld wanted without *really* breaking Smith's back? The solution: Make the rig for *two* men, hanging virtually in the same place—side by side, one almost on top of the other. Smith's head and torso would hang down on one side, where he could howl and struggle, in tremendous pain...but his legs would be up high, out of frame. The feet and legs that would appear in the frame would belong to Smith's stunt double, harnessed right there with him, while *his* torso sat up high, out of frame. CGI could then join the two bodies together in shadow, at the top of the visible picture, and it would look like Smith was being bent double, *backward,* and lived to tell the tale.

A New Kind of Subway Sandwich

The high-speed "Jeff the Worm" sequence that opens *MIB II* was a sandwich in more ways than one. It's an expert combination of computer graphics and practical effects, sandwiched together by top-flight editing, sound effects, and the Danny Elfman score.

But at the beginning, it was just Will Smith on the back of a blue-screen bucking bronco, a stuntman running through a window, and a specially built crane crushing a subway car—all on the California Sony lot, all carefully planned from front to back.

Since this would be Agent Jay's first appearance in the movie, and the first action sequence, the crew spent a lot of time getting his wild ride exactly right. Smith spent the better part of three days straddled on the blue-screen "back," hanging on for dear life to a small plastic flower, cabled up to bounce, and ultimately being flung off into space. Between takes, Smith was obviously wondering how his career had taken this odd turn. "This is what I do to feed my family," he said at one point. "Jumpin' around on a blue thing with a buncha dudes shakin' me."

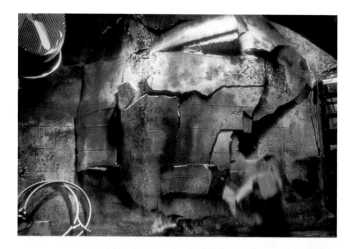

A NICE, OLD-FASHIONED EXPLOSION AND "REVEAL" OF THE BAD GUYS. ALMOST A NOVELTY IN THE MIDST OF ALL THIS COMPUTER-GENERATED STUFF.

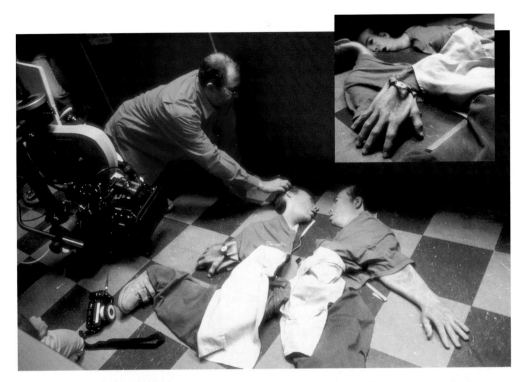

EVEN THE MOST "CASUAL" SORT OF TOSS-OFF IS THE RESULT OF HOURS OF PLANNING,

LEFT
PREPARATION AND DETAIL WORK. WHAT BEGAN AS VINCENT D'ONOFRIO'S FULL-BODY LIFECAST FOR EDGAR, GLIMPSED IN THE FIRST FEW SCENES OF *MEN IN BLACK*, REAPPEARS IN A WHOLLY DIFFERENT FORM, WITH NEW HAIR AND NEW CLOTHES.

BOTTOM LEFT AND RIGHT
THE DREADED BALLCHINIAN. A DISCREET HIGH COLLAR HIDES THE PUNCH LINE UNTIL—WELL, UNTIL IT GETS PUNCHED. BAD ENOUGH HE'S DOWNED BY A SINGLE BLOW...BUT TO LAND NEXT TO THE FERTILIZER SPREADERS! SUCH HUMILIATION!

CORNFACE SEEMS TO BE BENDING AGENT JAY IN HALF...

RIGHT AND CENTER
...WHEN IN FACT HE'S JUST BENDING WILL SMITH AND HIS STUNT DOUBLE IN QUARTERS (ONE QUARTER EACH). CHARLIE CROUGHWELL'S RIG LOOKS UNCOMFORTABLE, BUT NOT NEARLY AS UNCOMFORTABLE AS HAVING YOUR SPINE SNAPPED.

BELOW RIGHT
BARRY SONNENFELD EXPLAINS TO EVERYONE HOW YOU'RE *REALLY* SUPPOSED TO HANDLE A NOT-SO-TOUGH TENDRIL MAN.

BELOW LEFT
AGENT JAY IN AN UNCHARACTERISTIC MOMENT OF DIFFICULTY. GREG GARDINER AND CREW GO IN FOR A CLOSE-UP AS TENDRIL MAN WHOMPS HIM AROUND.

FLYING FROM WORM TO SUBWAY CAR IN ONE LEAP. "ORIGINALLY," SONNENFELD SAID, "THE WHOLE SEQUENCE OF WILL RIDING THE WORM WENT ON MUCH LONGER, BUT THEN IT WAS TURNING INTO TWO SCENES—WILL RIDING THE WORM, AND WILL IN THE SUBWAY CAR. IT'S MUCH BETTER AS *ONE* SCENE, A CHASE THAT ENDS WITH JEFF EATING THE SUBWAY CAR." BUT THAT MEANT CUTTING DOWN THE WORM-RIDING SIGNIFICANTLY, COLLAPSING ALL THE ACTION INTO A SINGLE HIGH-SPEED SEQUENCE. CHECK OUT THE MIKE RIGHT ABOVE WILL'S HEAD, SO THEY CAN CAPTURE AND USE HIS PANICKED SCREAM AS HE FLIES. THAT STARK TERROR STUFF IS *FUNNY*.

HE WAS ON THE WORM, THEN IN THE AIR. AND HERE HE COMES (OR RATHER HERE COMES RANDY LEROI, THE STUNT DOUBLE)...UNTIL THE LAST MINUTE, WHEN THEY PUT SMITH IN POSITION FOR THE LANDING.

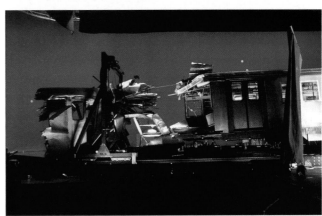

THIS SPECIAL RIG WAS MADE TO "CRUNCH" THE SUBWAY CAR IN JUST THE RIGHT PLACE. LATER, ILM'S COMPUTERIZED JEFF WILL COVER THE RIG COMPLETELY, SO THAT IT LOOKS AS IF THE GIANT (DIGITAL) WORM SNAPPED THE (PRACTICAL) SUBWAY CAR IN ITS TEETH.

BOTTOM
A PAUSE IN THE CATASTROPHE WHILE THE SUBWAY SET IS DRESSED TO LOOK *REALLY* TORN TO SHREDS.

RIGHT
...Then back to the action, as Agent Jay draws down on the rogue worm.

BELOW
Finally, the oblivious passengers step off the car, safe and sound...and nobody even remembers to say thank you to the Man in Black.

Not that he was finished. Just a few hours later he would be in a different rig, flying out into space as "Jeff" flung him free and sent him straight for the back window of a subway train.

Cut to the inside of the train...and watch as Smith's stunt double comes crashing through the specially prepared window of the subway door and executes a perfect tuck-and-roll amid all the flying glass, so Smith himself can come up, gun in hand, and confront the approaching worm.

Finally Smith was allowed to go off duty, while the *Men in Black* crew took a full-sized, very real New York subway car and fit it into a specially designed vise—a machine whose sole purpose was to crush the train as if it were in the jaws of a giant worm, pulling it apart like a sausage being bitten in half. Later the crushing machine would be covered completely by the computer-generated image of Jeff the Worm, mad as hell and not taking it anymore, as he tried to swallow the train in a single gulp.

The Big Finish

You have a rooftop. You have a big rock sculpture and a glass pyramid. And you have Will Smith trapped in the clutches of a giant, five-story-tall brambly organic creature who won't even be designed and animated for months to come.

What to do?

First: You blow up the pyramid. It's a great pyrotechnic effect, and it'll get an equally great, screeching sound to go with it when the sound is added.

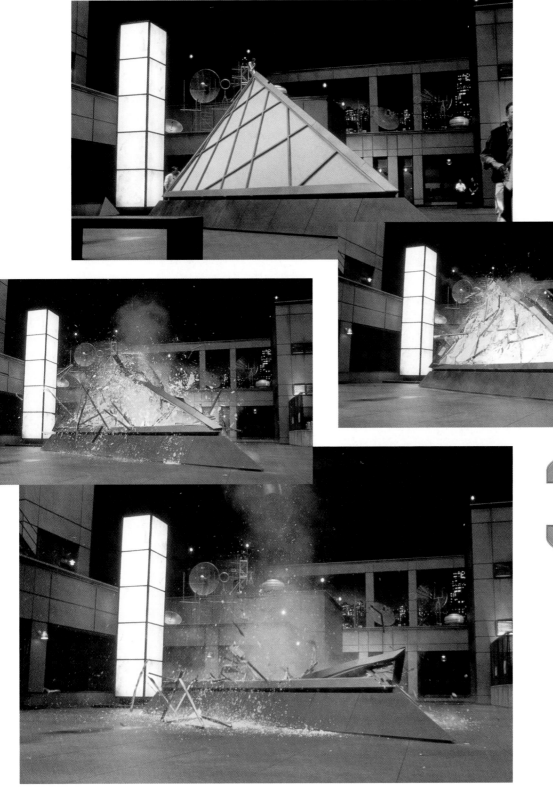

A SERIES OF SMALL, SMOKELESS CHARGES TURN THE PYRAMID TO SPLINTERS; THE SOUND EFFECTS, ADDED LATER, WILL MAKE IT SEEM MUCH BIGGER.

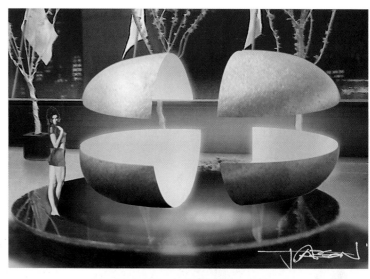

TOP
THE ART DEPARTMENT WENT
THROUGH COUNTLESS CONCEPT
DRAWINGS WHEN DETERMINING
HOW TO TURN THE ROCK SCULPTURE
INTO THE ROCK SHIP.

RIGHT
THE HIGHLY TECHNICAL,
IMMENSELY COMPLICATED CONVER-
SION PROCESS, LIVE AND ON
STAGE: WE STOP THE CAMERA. WE
PICK UP THE ROCK. WE MOVE IT.
WE PICK UP THE SHIP. WE MOVE
IT. WE START THE CAMERA AGAIN.
AMAZING, THESE SPECIAL EFFECTS!

CENTER
THE SHIP REPLACES THE STONE,
AND THINGS START GETTING EVEN
STRANGER.

ABOVE
WILL SMITH REHEARSING ON THE CARGO NET. PHYSICAL CHALLENGES LIKE THIS WERE EASY FOR SMITH; FRESH FROM THE *ALI* SHOOT, HE WAS IN TOP CONDITION (AND LOVING IT).

ABOVE LEFT
"**T**HIS WILL GIVE WILL ROOM TO PLAY," ILM'S JOHN BERTON SAID. "HE CAN DO WHATEVER HE WANTS; THERE'S LOTS OF ROOM FOR SPONTANEITY."

LEFT
ULTIMATELY, ILM WILL COVER MOST OF THE CARGO NET WITH THORNY SERLEENA TENDRILS, AND ERASE THE REST FROM VIEW.

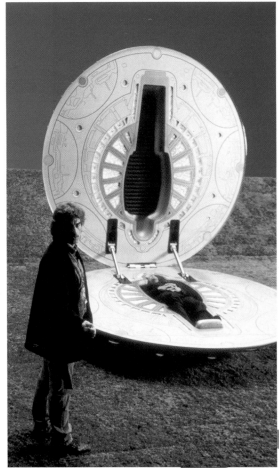

Welcome to
the travel pod.

Next stop:
Lockertown.

IN A STUNNING VISUAL
CREATED BY FRANCOIS AUDOUY,
THE ULTIMATE NEURALYZER
FLASHED ALL OF NEW YORK,
STRANGELY BEAUTIFUL AND
HOPEFUL IN LIGHT OF
ALL THAT'S HAPPENED....

Next: You stop the cameras long enough to roll out the rock sculpture and replace it with the Zarthan escape ship. In the final version, it will look as if a beam of light from the Statue of Liberty itself will have transformed the rock into the ship. But for the moment, it's going to take half a dozen stagehands to move the damn thing onstage.

Finally: John Berton of ILM and Stunt Coordinator Charlie Croughwell put their heads together and figure out what to do with Will Smith. They string a huge black cargo net across the entire length of the vast soundstage—the biggest around—and let Agent Jay go to town.

"This will give Will room to play," Berton said, for Jay will be swallowed alive by his gigantic foe. "He can do whatever he wants; there's lots of room for spontaneity, which helps the realism. And then we'll animate into that later."

They can easily get rid of all the cargo netting at the "wire removal" stage much later in the game. There have been major advances in the field—it's now possible to remove huge portions of a given image and still make it look and feel real. "It's easy this time, because we can shoot the clean backgrounds, and cover part of this with composites of the monster. It is possible to get rid of something as enormous as a big, flat cargo net and make it work for us."

DOSSIER

{#1703}

To: **Chief of Procurement V**
Transportation Division
MIB Office 4-834-4
From: **Director Zed**
Subject: **Current Vehicle Operation**
Parameters

UPGRADE TO MERCEDES-BENZ

Quite simply, *the Mercedes-Benz E500 is one of the most beautiful and beautifully made cars in the history of the world.*

There. It's out in the open.

In fact, the only thing that could possibly make the Mercedes-Benz E500 any cooler was if it could pull up its wheels and *fly*. But that's not possible, is it?

Is it?

In the world of *Men in Black II*, *anything* is possible...and a Mercedes-Benz with supersonic

capabilities is almost run-of-the-mill.

The work was split right down the middle: Industrial Light & Magic (ILM) would animate the exterior of the vehicle, according to designs originating in Bo Welch's Art Department. The interior would actually be built full sized, according to a separate set of specs, then be put on a gimballed rig in front of a blue-screen, where Jones, Smith, and Dawson would be tossed around like Ping-Pong balls in a basket. Then ILM would comp the two together to create the mad aerial chase across Manhattan that's a highlight of the last act.

It was exactly the same process that made the Ford LTD real in *Men in Black*...but the success of the "tunnel" sequence in the first film had

TOP LEFT: The interior of the "standard" Mercedes-Benz E500, though there's nothing standard about it.
LEFT: The interior of the unconverted MIB version of the Mercedes-Benz E500 (note the elliptical display).
ABOVE: The interior of the fully transformed and airborne Mercedes-Benz E500. Yow...

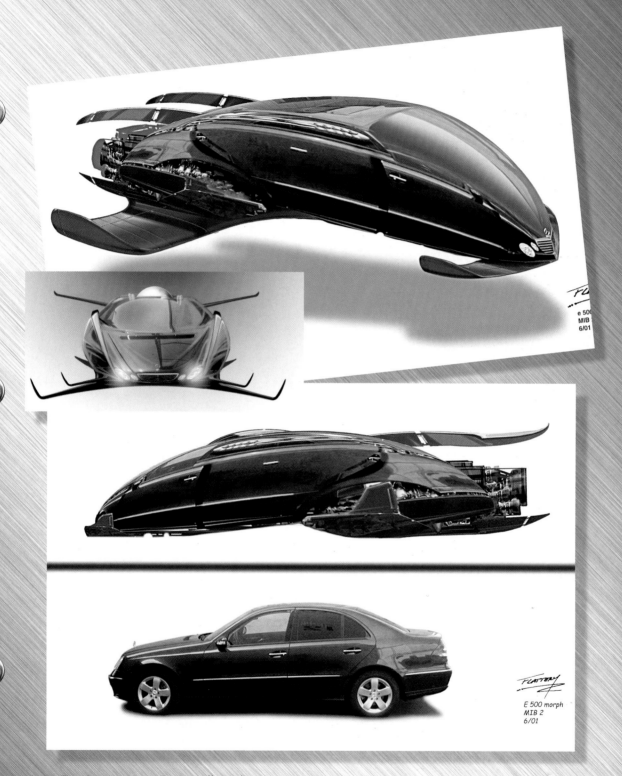

e 500
MIB 2
6/01

E 500 morph
MIB 2
6/01

ABOVE: The Mercedes-Benz E500 in all its glory, in different stages of concept development. Art by Tim Flattery

DOSSIER

raised the bar. For *Men in Black II*, everyone was expecting a cooler car, a bigger and better chase scene. So this *had* to work.

The conversion of the standard auto—as if there's anything *standard* about Mercedes-Benz and this work of automotive art—began with extensive reference photography, interior and exterior, at rest and in motion.

It was decided that the interior of the unconverted Mercedes-Benz would be only slightly modified. Instead of its standard AM/FM radio and CD player, there would be an elliptical display filled with MIB-like characters. The Art Department created the graphics that would go on the panel, and com-

plete renderings of the unconverted and converted interior—built directly on top of the reference photos, completely to scale—were prepared and approved, even by the folks at DaimlerChrysler.

The physical construction of the interior required a series of plans from 3D Model Maker Paul Ozzimo, among many others. Then the prop crew had to build a very tough, structurally sound "capsule" that could take the jolting and jostling of the

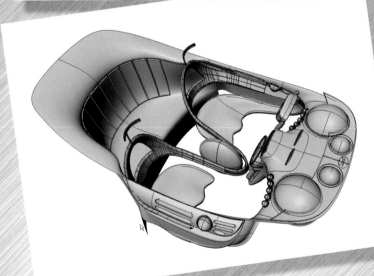

ABOVE: The Art Department even designed the look and text for the Mercedes-Benz readouts.
LEFT: Paul Ozzimo created a 3D model of the "capsule."
TOP LEFT: The capsule itself was made of plastic, steel, and foam—strong enough to withstand a whole lotta shakin' goin' on.

The rolling, dipping, and tipping of the blue-screen shoot should have been your basic SFX nightmare, but once again Will Smith made it almost bearable.

gimballed rig. This thing had to be *strong*—it had to hold three grown humans and turn them all completely upside down for a *long* time—and it had to do it so smoothly that audiences would really believe they were airborne. The final construct was a combination of steel, molded plastic, fiberglass, and fabric...and it held up admirably despite all the stress.

The blue-screen shoot itself was a physical challenge, but (as always) Will Smith kept it light. With an endless series of improvs, he made it his personal mission to make Tommy Lee Jones crack up...not just once, but over and over. It took a while, but he succeeded. More than once, they had to take a break just to give the actors a chance to wipe the tears out of their eyes and compose themselves.

It was just *way* too much fun, on a day that should have been a visit to Soundstage Hell.

The final composited effect is one of the highlights of *Men in Black II*. The converted exterior of the Mercedes-Benz E500 is a natural extrapolation of the sleek aerodynamic lines and supple shapes of the real car, and the conversion process itself is awe-inspiring. The "new" version doesn't look remade or tricked out; it looks *evolved*—a whole new automotive art form. And it really *does* look like it can fly.

The interior is positively dazzling: The console is a mass of shimmering domes and readouts; the steering wheel is replaced by a stalk-like steering device. So when it finally happens, when Agent Jay pushes the red button and the Mercedes-Benz E500 finally takes to the air, you *believe* it...and the only question in the minds of viewers the world over is, *Where can I buy one?*

A MARRIAGE MADE IN DIGITAL HEAVEN

CHAPTER 3

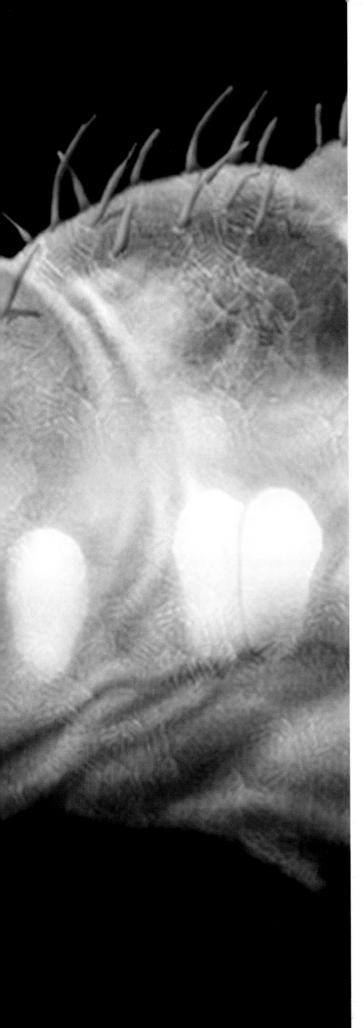

John Berton, the visual effects supervisor from Industrial Light & Magic, had been watching the progress on *MIB II* from the very beginning. The entire time, he knew he had a heck of a challenge ahead of him, but he welcomed it. He knew what his job was...and what his job was *not*.

"This movie is not about the visual effects," he explained. "The visual effects play a very important role, but people aren't going to go see a movie like *Men in Black* just to see the visual effects. They're going to see something that's of a much larger scope, and something much more sophisticated than that. The integration of the visual effects into the overall plan must be as subtle as the comedy that's played through it, and the drama that's played through it, and the characters that are played through it. That's an important thing to understand."

That was why he made sure he was on the set from the very beginning—to understand what *MIB II* is *about*, so he would be prepared to lead the team at ILM in creating visual effects that match it in style and substance. "You can only get that if you've got somebody who's there as it's coming together," he said. "As the movie is being created on the set, it's very important to understand what the film is all about, where the director is going with it, what the screenwriter intended—all that goes into it, especially in tone."

In the first months of 2002, long after principal photography had ended and Rick Baker's work as a monster maker had been completed, Berton and his crew—Art Director David Nakabayashi and a host of others—began the arduous task of adding in and taking out the elements that the script and the live photography called for.

They would have to evolve three separate looks for Serleena: her initial transformation into a Victoria's Secret model at the beginning of the picture; her neural root takeover of MIB HQ in the middle of the picture; and her final transformation into the gnarly monster that nearly eats Jay, until Scrad's proton bomb blows her to kingdom come. They were three related but distinct projects...and they were all going to be very tough.

This wasn't working in a vacuum, though. Since the very beginning, Berton had worked with Sonnenfeld, Baker, and Bo Welch. "They're the ones who are really setting the visual style

JEFF THE WORM MAY BE THE ULTIMATE SONNENFELD/BAKER DESIGN. WITH MOUTH CLOSED, HE LOOKS ALMOST HARMLESS, AND A LITTLE BIT GOOFY—CECIL THE SEA SERPENT AFTER A HARD NIGHT ON THE TOWN...

...BUT HE OPENS HIS MOUTH, AND *YIKES!*
ART BY CHRISTIAN ALZMANN (ILM)

for the film," he said. "We draw everything from that. We have a great many talented people working here at ILM, of course, and Rick Baker's shop, Cinovation, is incredible—we have huge respect for him, and he's basically the point man for Bo and Barry when it comes to the aliens." The ILM team worked on a wide variety of designs—Jarra and his mini creatures, the transformations of the Mercedes-Benz E500, a number of aliens. "But all that goes back to Bo," he observed. "Bo is the person who's designing the film, that's his job, and we want to make sure that everything we do is definitely within the parameters that fit in with the rest of production. Though we really love to go ahead and flesh out our ideas—and it's great to work with people like Barry and Bo, who let us do that."

And the challenge involved a lot more than creating creatures that appeared on screen. "There's been a tremendous number of drawings," Berton said. "For every creature that appears in the movie, there's probably fifty drawings that we do, of which maybe fifteen will be selected out and then shown to Rick and to Barry. Those will eventually get honed down to three or four creatures that we really like."

And nowhere has the challenge been greater than with the biggest creature of all, Jeff the Worm.

"We had a better idea of what he was going to be like from the very beginning," Berton said, "but the look and lighting—how he will actually look on the screen—has actually gone through an enormous amount of iteration. We did almost all the original creature design, but getting his face to look right, and getting his eyes to be someplace where they can be used as an expressive element within the tight confines of the sequence...that required a great deal of collaboration from everyone. We would do our designs, and we'd run 'em by Rick, who would paint on our images in his computer, and then we'd take them back to show them to Barry, and Barry would make the adjustments he felt were necessary. And we'd come back and rebuild that into the full worm, and we'd run that by Rick again, and Rick would look at what he needed to change to maintain his idea, and then back to Barry...It sounds convoluted, but that's the only way you really get something that's perfect for the movie."

Visual design was one task—and a *big* one, both for ILM and for the creative team in L.A.—but ILM had another, equally important responsibility: *pulling the visuals together*—integrating live action, practical effects, and computer-generated effects into a series of seamless events.

"What's great about a lot of the things that happen in the *MIB* movies is the combination of different techniques [appearing] in a single frame," Berton said. "A lot of what you see with visual effects is that way, and to me, it's one of the most effective ways to work. Here you've got Will Smith and his tremendous physical

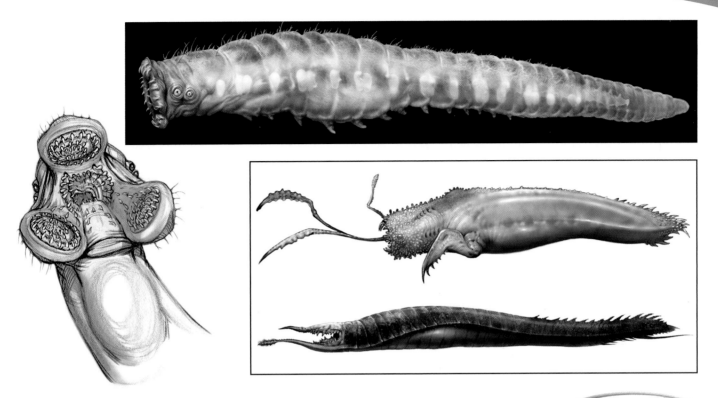

performance as the foundation of everything you're doing. Then you layer in a great-looking creature that could not exist in reality, at least as we know it, and now you've got a synthesis happening on the screen, and that's what really sings. If you put just a big ol' CG creature on the screen, okay, that's got some spectacular nature to it, but it doesn't draw you in by itself. But you take Will Smith and you put him on its back and have him start to perform…then you're drawn in, you've got a human being pulling you into that moment. That's what we always try to build, and that's what the visual effects are really doing in this movie—supporting the main agenda, which is the journey of our heroes through the story.

"It's a challenge," Berton admitted, "but one that I accept gladly. At the moment we have a three-hundred-foot worm bursting through the sidewalk, as we have in this movie, we don't want people in the audience to go, 'Whoa, cool CG.' We want the audience to be going, *'YIII! Huge worm! Run for your lives!'* Keeping the suspension of disbelief alive is really critical, especially when it comes to *MIB II*, where the audience is part of the MIB world."

And because this is a sequel, the ILM folks faced a particularly difficult task. "We have a tremendous foundation on which to build, but that also means we've had a standard set for us about how to proceed with the postproduction. There are no excuses: We know that the production footage is great, we know the actors are really on the mark; now it's up to us to make sure that the visual effects meet that same standard.

"If everybody's doing the right thing, it all works together and we end up with a great film."

THE MANY FACES (AND BODIES) OF JEFF THE WORM

"WE HAD A GOOD IDEA OF WHAT JEFF WAS GOING TO BE LIKE FROM THE VERY BEGINNING," JOHN BERTON SAID, "BUT THE LOOK AND LIGHTING—HOW HE WILL ACTUALLY LOOK ON THE SCREEN—HAS ACTUALLY GONE THROUGH A TREMENDOUS AMOUNT OF ITERATION." HERE ARE JUST A FEW OF THE VARIATIONS ON A THEME. ART BY CHRISTIAN ALZMANN (TOP AND FAR LEFT), CARLOS HUANTE (BOXED ART, TOP), AND CARLOS HUANTE AND RANDY GAUL (BOXED ART, BOTTOM). ALL ARTISTS FROM ILM.

When Jeff finally catches up with Jay in the last car, the results are dramatic, to say the least!

DOSSIER
#9382

To: **Tracking Department**
CC: **Alien Tracking**
           Security & Enforcement
           Hazmat Cleanup Planning and
           Procedures
           Mnemonic Design and
           Manipulation
           Personnel
           ALL Offices and Field Stations
From: **Zed**
Subject: **Missing Extraterrestrials**

THE LOST ALIENS OF RICK BAKER

"I have done more drawings for this picture," Rick Baker said, "than I have done for all the other movies I've ever done in my career...combined."

The problem is that there simply wasn't enough room for all of them, and sadly, some of his fondest work barely survives at all. For instance, untold hours

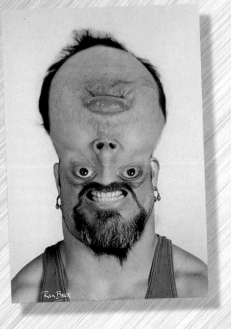

DOSSIER

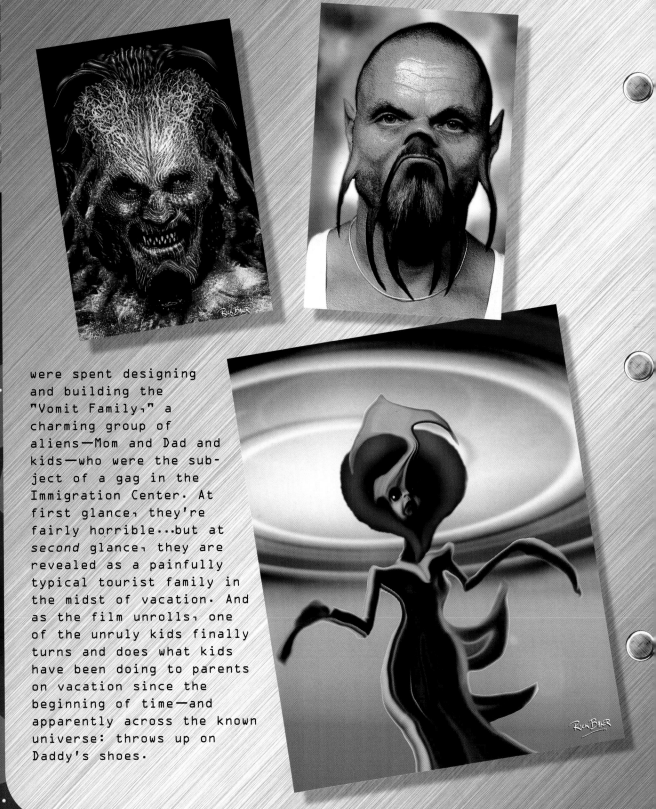

were spent designing
and building the
"Vomit Family," a
charming group of
aliens—Mom and Dad and
kids—who were the sub-
ject of a gag in the
Immigration Center. At
first glance, they're
fairly horrible...but at
second glance, they are
revealed as a painfully
typical tourist family in
the midst of vacation. And
as the film unrolls, one
of the unruly kids finally
turns and does what kids
have been doing to parents
on vacation since the
beginning of time—and
apparently across the known
universe: throws up on
Daddy's shoes.

It was a great bit, everybody agreed, but in the final cut, Barry Sonnenfeld had to move the action along; too much time was being spent in Men in Black HQ when there was a story to tell. So the Vomit Family—along with plenty of other *very* cool aliens—were reduced to silent subjects in a quick dolly shot.

Other equally wonderful alien creations from Rick Baker never got past the concept stage. "It's my only problem with this movie," Baker said. "There just aren't enough aliens."

Here, then, are a few of the really great aliens that Rick Baker designed but never made it all the way to the set....

MIIB™
MEN IN BLACK II
THE SCREENPLAY

BASED ON THE SCEENPLAY BY ROBERT GORDON
AND BARRY FANARO. STORY BY ROBERT GORDON.

TITLE SEQUENCE

A SPACECRAFT

blasts through a black star-filled sky, blowing up planets as it roars toward...EARTH.

EXT. CENTRAL PARK—NIGHT

A GOLDEN RETRIEVER is staring up at the night sky, BARKING. A FAT MAN runs up out of breath.

MAN Harvey...*heel.*

He tries to get the dog to stop, but Harvey won't budge.

MAN You're barking at the moon, moron.

The dog pulls away.

THE SPACECRAFT swoops in from the exact direction Harvey was looking. It lands in front of a grassy hillside.

PUSH IN ON: THE SPACECRAFT

A ramp lowers. A small NEURAL ROOT CREATURE, in shadows, slithers off the spacecraft. After a beat, Harvey runs back and barks at the NEURAL ROOT CREATURE.

MAN (o.c.) Harvey!

We now see the SPACECRAFT is less than TWO FEET ACROSS. THE SMALL CREATURE Harvey is barking at rises up and makes a horrible sound. Harvey runs off whimpering.

Leaves and pages from a newspaper blow by. The creature makes its way to a New York Magazine *lying on the ground. "I Love NY" on the cover.*

The CREATURE spews a glob of blue spittle on the magazine's cover. The wind blows the magazine open to an advertisement.

The CREATURE checks out the picture. Suddenly, the small root BLOOMS—spindly, hair-like membranes turn back on themselves, multiplying. The blooming roots begin to take shape and form. An undulating leg, torso, arm, hand...

ANGLE ON:

A Victoria's Secret lingerie ad. A BEAUTIFUL MODEL in BLACK LIN-GERIE poses provocatively.

We follow up to—THE BEAUTIFUL VICTORIA'S SECRET MODEL who looks at "her" picture in the magazine. This is SERLEENA.

Out of nowhere, A KNIFE appears against her throat.

MAN'S VOICE (o.c.) Hey, pretty lady.

The woman glances over her shoulder to see—A CREEP in a long, black leather coat.

CREEP Umm, you taste good.

He licks her neck and then pulls her behind some trees.

CREEP (o.c.) *(yelling)* Hey! What the...?!

Serleena reaches back, picks him up over her head and SWALLOWS HIM WHOLE.

SERLEENA Yeah, you too.

Serleena looks down at her stomach...now A BIG BEER BELLY from eating the creep. She looks at the model's impossibly flat stomach in the magazine. Serleena walks over to some bushes, puts her finger down her throat and retches OFF CAMERA. She crosses out of the bushes, admiring her totally flat model stomach.

She reaches down and picks up the creep's leather coat and boots and crosses off into the darkness.

EXT. STEAM GRATE—NIGHT

FIREFLY'S POV

A BEAUTIFUL FLOWER on the end of a delicate stalk—sticking straight out of the steam grate.

TWO SETS OF BLACK SHOES walk into frame. As they cross to the flower...

The SECOND FIGURE, AGENT TEE, speaks.

TEE (o.c.) You want me to shake him down? Teach him a thing or two. Let him know who's in charge.
JAY Nothing fancy, no heroics. By the book this time.
TEE Got it.

Tee gives the flower a tap with his shoe. The flower goes rigid.

JAY (o.c.) Hey, Jeff. What's happening, buddy? We were just wondering what you were doing here.

Nothing. He gives the flower another tap.

TEE (o.c.) The man's talking to you.
JAY (o.c.) You know our arrangement, Jeff. You don't travel outside of the E, F, and R subway lines and in exchange, you get to eat all the non-organic garbage you want.

Tee's hand reaches in and grabs the delicate little flower's stalk.

.....WE BOOM UP TO REVEAL OUT OF BREATH GUY.....

.....SAYING HIS LINES.

SINGLE - DOG BARKING.....

.....IT SITS UP AND MAKES A HORRIBLE SOUND AT THE DOG.

.....WITH BUSH'S FACE ON THE COVER.

SIDE < TRACKING SHOT OF WORM.....

WORM'S POV OF BUSH'S FACE - HOLD ON IT.....

.....WIND BLOWS THE PAGES OF THE MAGAZINE.....

.....REVEALING VICTORIA'S SECRET MODEL.

.....THE WORM WATCHES THE PAGES TURN, AND THEN CHECKS OUT VICTORIA'S SECRET MODEL.....

.....IT BEGINS TO SPROUT LITTLE FEELERS,.....

.....WE TILT AND BOOM UP.....

.....WE TILT AND BOOM UP.....

.....SUDDENLY AN ARM REACHES INTO FRAME AROUND HER NECK AND PULLS HER OUT OF SHOT.

.....[TRACKING WITH THEM] HE LICKS HER NECK AS HE KEEPS MOVING TOWARDS THE BUSHES.....

.....THEY DISAPPEAR BEHIND THE BUSHES.

POP IN C/U OF CREEP LICKING SERLEENA'S NECK.

.....SHE LOOKS LOWER, AT HER STOMACH.....

TEE (O.C.) What are you doing here, wormboy?

The ground trembles.

JAY (O.C.) *(yells to Tee)* Tee!
(to Jeff) Jeff, excuse my partner! He's new and he's...

A HUGE, WORM-LIKE CREATURE emerges from under the street. He's angrily trying to shake off Tee—who is holding on for dear life to the thin stalk and flower growing out of JEFF'S ugly head.

JEFF rears back and catapults Tee off with such force...he disappears high into the night sky.

TEE Ahhhhh...

PUSH IN ON: JAY, looking up.

JAY ...kind of stupid.

Jeff slowly slinks down, face-to-face with Jay.

JAY Getting big, Jeff. What've you been eating?

Jeffrey's SPIKY TAIL BURSTS up through the pavement behind Jay and WHIP-CRACKS him across the street. He crashes into a FRUIT STAND.

Jay sees Jeff slithering back in the hole.

JAY Jeffrey!

Jay jumps in the hole...

INT. SUBWAY TUNNEL—NIGHT—CONTINUOUS

Jeff is there. Jay lands on top of him.

The worm races off with Jay hanging onto his back.

JEFF slams his head...and Jay's...against the top of the tunnel.

Jay takes out a long metal cylinder. He sticks the air-compressed syringe in the "flower." PSSHT...

JAY Sweet dreams, big boy.

JEFF BOLTS down the subway tunnel with Jay on his back.

INT. PRINCE STREET SUBWAY STATION—NIGHT

People wait for their train.

AN EXPRESS TRAIN zooms through the station with a deafening clatter. People glance up, then go back to their newspapers.

THE GIANT SCREECHING WORM, WITH JAY RIDING ON HIS BACK, rockets through the station. People glance up—go back to

their papers—THEN LOOK UP AGAIN.

INT. SUBWAY TUNNEL—NIGHT—CONTINUOUS

Jay rides the worm like it was some intergalactic bucking bronc.

JAY Sweet dreams...

Jay is flung onto the car.

JAY (CONT'D) ...big boy!

INT. SUBWAY TUNNEL—NIGHT

Jeff snaps his head, flinging Jay onto the last car of a SUBWAY TRAIN traveling on the track ahead of them.

Jay looks back. Jeff is following.

INT. SUBWAY CAR—NIGHT—CONTINUOUS

Jay enters.

JAY Transit Authority, people. Please move to the forward car. We got a bug in the electrical system.

The handful of passengers completely ignore him.

JAY YO! PEOPLE!

They look up.

JAY We got a bug in the electrical system!

Jay nods to the back door. GIANT SNAPPING WORM JAWS. SCREAMS as everyone runs to the next car.

Crunch. Jeff takes a bite from the last 20 feet of train.

INT. NEXT CAR

People rush through in complete hysteria.

JAY No, no. Sit down. It's only a 600-foot worm!

No one's asking questions. Everyone gets up and follows the others.

INT. SUBWAY CAR—NIGHT

Jay looks back to see the WORM CRUNCHING DOWN on the last subway car.

JAY Go! Go! Go! Just scream one more time!

Jay RUNS FROM CAR TO CAR—a furious race to keep ahead of the worm who is eating each car as it's abandoned.

INT. CONDUCTOR'S CAR—NIGHT

.....THE FIREFLY ENTERS, IT BECOMES OTS OVER THE FIREFLY ONTO THE FLOWER.....

.....AND APPROACHES A THIRD TIME.

.....SHINNY SHOES GET OUT .....

MODIFIED OTS OVER THE FLOWER ONTO THE SHOES- WIDER LENS,.....

..... THE OTHER PAIR OF SHOES BACK UP, OFF THE GRATING.....

..... A CG JEFF BURSTS THROUGHT THE FRAME.....

CLOSE UP ON STREET PERSON

.....JEFF FLINGS A CG T WAY INTO THE NIGHT SKY, SILHOUETTED BY A FULL MOON.

ANGLE ON GRATING.

.....JEFF FLOPS DOWN INTO FRAME, HIS HEAD AND FLOWER LOOKING UP AT J, ...

..... THEN HE DROPS DOWN INTO THE HOLE.

LOW < LOOKING DOWN AT JEFF- AFTER FLIPPING OFF T.

.... JEFF'S TAIL BURSTS THROUGH THE PAVEMENT IN THE BG.....

..... AND SWIPES J OFF CAMERA RIGHT.

ANGLE ON J - LANDING ON OLD BENCH.....

.....AND EXITS FRAME.

LOW < FROM INSIDE THE HOLE- J ENTERS FRAME, HAVING BEEN SWIPED BY JEFF'S TAIL,.....

..... AND JUMPS INTO THE HOLE.

The door is flung open and THIRTY SCREAMING PEOPLE enter.

MOTORMAN Everybody out before I start knockin' heads here.
JAY You get in there and you put the hammer down on this thing.
MOTORMAN I'm Captain Larry Bridgewater and I decide what happens on this train.
JAY Oh. You decide? Okay, come here.

Jay puts his arm around Larry's neck, pulls him over.

JAY Larry? Meet my man, Jeff.

We hear a SCREECH—Larry turns to see JEFF MUNCHING the last car behind them.

MOTORMAN Larry just made a decision.
JAY Yeah, Larry can get his ass in there.

The conductor THROWS down the THROTTLE.

INT. SUBWAY CAR—NIGHT

THE WORM'S JAWS SNAP at the conductor's car, ripping a huge piece of aluminum off the back. They can see down the WORM'S HOT GULLET. SCREAMS.

Jay raises his gun and just as he's about to fire—

JAY Don't make me do this, Jeff!

JEFF CLOSES HIS MOUTH, finally passes out, and the train keeps moving on.

INT. 81ST STREET STATION—NIGHT

The mangled conductor's car—half on the track, half off—limps pathetically into the station and squeaks to a stop.

INT. CONDUCTOR'S CAR—NIGHT

JAY 81st Street.

He puts on his Ray•Bans and holds up his neuralyzer.

JAY May I have your attention please...

FLASH...Everyone is bathed in the light.

JAY The City of New York would like to thank you for participating in our drill. Had this been an actual emergency, you all would have been eaten. Because you don't listen. You're hardheaded. That's the problem with all you New Yorkers. Explain to me how a man's going to come bashing through the back of a subway window, ask you all nicely to move, and you...

Jay holds up his neuralyzer again.

JAY Thank you for participating in our drill. Hopefully you enjoyed our new, smaller, more energy-efficient subway cars. Watch your step. You will have a nice evening.

INT. 81ST STREET STATION—NIGHT

Neuralyzer flash. Everyone calmly files out as if nothing ever happened. Jay walks out talking into his communicator...

JAY I need the perimeter secured and a clean-up crew at 81st and Central Park West.

Several seconds pass, then DOZENS OF MEN IN BLACK SUITS swarm in through the entrances and go about their business.

JAY Revoke Jeff's movement privileges immediately, have a Transfer Team escort him back to the Chambers Street Station...and could somebody please check the expiration date on the unipod worm tranquilizers.

EXT. 81ST STREET STATION—NIGHT—MOMENTS LATER

Jay comes up the subway stairs. The subway entrance has been roped off.

JAY Sorry, fellas. Station closed. Emergency drill for your safety.
NEW YORK GUY *(to his friend)* You believe these putzes?

The two guys walk off.

JAY You're welcome.

Jay walks over and takes a seat on a bench. The ROSE PLANETARIUM is behind him. After a beat he moves over and Tee lands with a thud where Jay was sitting.

TEE I know. By the book.

Jay stares up at the night sky.

JAY Tee, when was the last time we just...looked at the stars?
TEE If this is a test, I can do this.
JAY Ever feel like you're alone in the universe?
TEE Yes.

Jay looks at him.

TEE No.

Jay gets up.

JAY Hey, let me buy you a piece of pie.
TEE Really? Thanks.

As they head up the street, Tee puts his arm around Jay's shoulder.

TEE Hey, you're not alone in the universe.
JAY Remove the arm, Tee. Okay.

INT. SCRAD'S APARTMENT—NIGHT

A dump filled with pop culture junk and piles of magazines that sell it. SCRAD enters wearing a backpack. Like many New Yorkers, he starts screaming, at no one.

.....AND LANDS ON JEFF'S BACK, ...
LONG SPEECH.....

.... WE HOLD FOR A FEW SECONDS, THEN JAY JUMPS FROM JEFF
TOWARDS THE BACK OF THE TRAIN.

.....AND REACTING TO JEFF EATING THE BACK 1/4 OF THE SUBWAY CAR.

.....SHOT BECOMES AN OTS OVER THE FLOWER ONTO JAY.....

.....HE CRASHES THROUGH THE WINDOW.....

JAY'S POV OF JEFF.....

C/U JEFF'S EYES - HE CONSIDERS IT.....

INSIDE THE CAR - JAY CRASHES THROUGH THE WINDOW.....

SIDE OF JEFF AND THE TRAIN, WE SEE PEOPLE SCURRYING
FROM CAR TO CAR.

.....AND STICKS IT INTO FLOWER.....

.....WE PULL JAY AS HE MAKES SPEECH ABOUT MOVING TO THE
FRONT CAR.

.....JAY TAKES OUT HIS GUN AND POINTS IT AT THE ENGINEER JUST
AS ANOTHER BITE IS TAKEN OUT OF THE BACK OF THE TRAIN

PULLING WIDE < - SEE JEFF'S FACE AND JAY SMALL ON HIS BACK.

.....THEY SEE JEFF CRUNCHING THE SUBWAY CAR OFF
CAMERA

.....ENGINEER LARRY ENTERS AND PUTS THE PEDAL TO THE MEDAL.

SIDE WIDE < TRACKING SHOT - JEFF WITH JAY ON HIS
BACK TRAVELLING LEFT TO RIGHT.....

.....BEHIND HIM - THE WHOLE BACK 1/4 OF THE SUBWAY CAR
IS BITTEN OFF, REVEALING JEFF AND ALL HIS TEETH

PULLING JEFF - HE GOES FROM ANGRY.....

SCRAD Shut up, Charlie! I'm tired of you constantly talking behind my back.

He opens the refrigerator, which partially BLOCKS HIS FACE.

SCRAD *(takes out a bottle)* Only one beer left.
DIFFERENT VOICE What about me?
SCRAD Shut up. I'll share.
DIFFERENT VOICE Forget it. I know where your mouth's been.

He shuts the door of the fridge.

SCRAD Fine.

Scrad turns to see SERLEENA standing right next to him.

SCRAD *(startled)* Whoa!

Scrad drops his beer bottle, which smashes on the floor. He looks up at Serleena. She's fashioned a weird but sexy outfit from the Central Park creep's leather coat.

SCRAD Wh-Who are you? And how'd you get in here?...

A HEAD pops out of Scrad's backpack, attached to Scrad's shoulders. This head is CHARLIE —the other voice. He checks out Serleena.

CHARLIE Any interest in a ménage à trois?

NEURAL ROOTS extend from her fingers and wrap around Scrad's and Charlie's necks.

CHARLIE *(choking)* Kinky.
SCRAD *(choking)* Ser-leena! Why—didn't—you say—it was you?

Serleena looks around the apartment taking in all the trappings of Earth with disdain.

SERLEENA High Definition TV...Internet...PlayStation 2...

She grabs a magazine and holds it up to their faces.

SERLEENA Entertainment Weekly?

BRAD PITT and ED NORTON are on the cover.

SERLEENA I hired you to find the Light and you go Earthling?

They hang their heads in shame.

SCRAD We hate Earth.

Charlie's head accordions up behind Scrad.

CHARLIE We're just trying to fit in.
SERLEENA You have the information?
SCRAD Information?
SERLEENA I sent you an interstellar fax.

CHARLIE Fax. Toner cartridge went bad. You try to find a replacement for a Kylothian...

Roots shoot out of her fingers and into their ears.

SERLEENA Yes or no?
SCRAD/CHARLIE AHHH!
SCRAD AHH!
CHARLIE AHH!
SCRAD/CHARLIE AHHHHHH!!!!
SCRAD *(as fast as he can get it out)* We couldn't find the Light—but we tracked it to a guy who might know where it is. He runs a pizza parlor on Spring Street.

The neural roots disappear into her hands.

SERLEENA Well, let's go.

She exits.

Scrad and Charlie stand, trying to catch their breath from the excruciating pain.

CHARLIE We're gonna miss, *Friends.*
SCRAD Shut up.
CHARLIE Pleeeeeaaase.

Scrad crosses to the door. He runs back and hits a button on a machine. As he runs out...

SCRAD Tivo.
CHARLIE Beauty, Scrad.

EXT. DINER—NIGHT—ESTABLISHING

A small, neighborhood diner. A taxi cruises.

INT. DINER—NIGHT

Jay sits across from Tee. They're having coffee and pie. Long beat of awkward silence, then...

TEE Oh, good pie.
JAY Yeah.
TEE Crowded.
JAY They got good pie.

Tee starts crying.

JAY Man, what is wrong with you?
TEE You're gonna neuralyze me.
JAY No I'm not.
TEE Yes you are. You took me to a public place so I wouldn't make a scene.
JAY You are making a scene.

INT. SCRAD'S APT. - CAMERA, BLOCKED BY JUNK, TRACKS TO REVEAL..... *cont'd*

.....SCRAD COMING IN THROUGH THE DOOR.....

.....AS HE GETS TO THE FRIDGE.....

.....SCRAD TURNS TOWARDS THE LENS AND DROPS HIS BEER.

.... AND BREAKS.

.....AS SHE PICKS UP STUFF, ETC.

.....NEURAL ROOT EXTENDS FROM SERLEENA AND OUT OF SHOT..... *cont'd*

.....NEURAL ROOT COMES BACK INTO SHOT..... *cont'd*

OVER SCRAD AND CHARLIE'S SHOULDERS ONTO SERLEENA..... *cont'd*

.....NEURAL ROOT COMES OUT OF SERLEENA AND WRAPS AROUND THEIR NECKS.

TWO SHOT - CHARLIE AND SCRAD'S HEADS

OVER SERLEENA ONTO SCRAD AND CHARLIE- CG NEURAL ROOTS IN THEIR EARS.

PICK UP TWO SHOT OF CHARLIE AND SCRAD- NEURAL ROOTS LET GO OF THEIR HEADS..... *cont'd*

... WE PAN CHARLIE PARTWAY OUT, STAYING ON SHOT OF T.V. *cont'd*

.....SCRAD COMES BACK INTO FRAME AND PUTS A TAPE IN THE VCR..... *cont'd*

.....AND EXITS.

Half the restaurant turns to look.

JAY *(leans in)* Hey, how long have we been partners?
TEE Feb. 1.

ANGLE ON: Jay's hands under the table. He's dialing his neuralyzer.

JAY So five months and three days...
TEE ...started at noon.
JAY ...nine hours.

Jay can't take it anymore. He takes out his neuralyzer. FLASH.

JAY Get married. Have a bunch of kids.
TEE Okay.

Jay gets up and crosses by a PRETTY WAITRESS on his way out the door...

JAY Excuse me. My buddy's kinda shy, but he thinks you are hot.

He points to Tee who is staring into space and exits.

EXT. BEN'S FAMOUS PIZZA (OF SOHO)—NIGHT—ESTABLISHING

A small, neighborhood pizzeria. A taxi cruises by.

INT. BEN'S FAMOUS PIZZA (OF SOHO)—NIGHT

Laura enters, carrying two cases of soft drinks. She's about to call out to BEN...when she hears arguing from the front. She quietly closes the door behind her.

SERLEENA (o.s.) Two slices of pepperoni and any information you might have about the Light of Zartha.
BEN Please. Whoever you are...don't hurt me.

Laura cracks the door to the kitchen. She sees Serleena and Scrad working over Ben.

SERLEENA Where is the Light, "Ben"?
BEN I don't know what you're talking about. Please let me down, ma'am.

Serleena puts her hand around Ben's throat. Laura grabs the wall phone and dials 911.

LAURA Hello? I want to report a robbery at...

She hears a SQUEAKING sound and turns to see the back door ajar, being blown open by the wind. BANG. It bounces against the wall.

Scrad and Serleena hear the noise. Serleena motions for Scrad to check it out.

SERLEENA There! Noise! Kitchen!
CHARLIE Oh, right.

He goes to check it out.

Scrad enters and looks around. Nothing. He sees the back door open.

We see him crossing to close the door—from Laura's POV—hidden in a cabinet under the sink.

SERLEENA (o.c.) You idiots see anything?
SCRAD The wind blew the door open.

Charlie's head pops out of the backpack.

CHARLIE Nothing outta the ordinary.

Laura's eyes widen. Scrad closes the door and heads to the front. When he gets to the door, he whips around to check out the room. Nothing. As Scrad turns around, Charlie's head whips back for one last look. They exit.

Laura pokes her head out of the cabinet. She can see Ben, Serleena, and Scrad/Charlie.

Serleena puts her neural root finger on Ben's face and lifts him up.

SERLEENA For twenty-five years I've traveled the universe looking for the Light...but it never left Earth, did it, "Ben"? You kept it here.
BEN What are you talking about?
SERLEENA I'm running out of time. Where's the Light of Zartha?
BEN I-I swear I don't know what you're talking about...
SERLEENA Listen, son, you hid the Light on Earth and I will find it. Once we have the Light, Zartha will be ours.
BEN You're too late. Tomorrow the Light will leave the third planet and be back home...Sorry you made the trip for nothing.

Serleena cracks her whip and RIPS Ben open. His humanoid skin drops in a heap on the floor.

Alien Ben EXPLODES and cracks into THOUSANDS OF PHOSPHO-RESCENT PIECES.

CHARLIE Got nothing out of him. Now we don't know if it's on Earth or not.
SERLEENA He said, *Third Planet.* It's here, you idiot!
SCRAD *(whispers)* Third Rock from the Sun.
CHARLIE *(whispers)* I never got that till now.
SERLEENA It's on Earth, and I know who's gonna tell me where it is.
(beat)
Time to visit my old friend Kay.

Serleena walks off with a pizza in her hand, stepping on Ben on the way out. Scrad/Charlie follow.

PUSH IN ON: Laura. Her knees are pulled to her chest. She's shaking and crying. She looks up at the skylight. RAIN.

EXT. MIB HEADQUARTERS—NIGHT—ESTABLISHING

INT. MIB ENTRANCE—NIGHT—AT THE SAME TIME

HIGH OVERHEAD. Jay enters. As he passes the OLD SECURITY GUARD on his way to the elevator.

SECURITY GUARD *(buried behind his paper)* Don't you ever go home?

INT. PIZZERIA - TWO SHOT FROM MARIA'S POV OF SERLEENA AND BEN. SCRAD STANDS IN B/G.....
cont'd

.....PART OF SERLEENA'S BODY OVERLAPS MITCHES, IT LOOKS TO MARIA THAT BEN IS PICKED UP BY SERLEENA'S HANDS.....
cont'd

REVERSE < - PROFILE ON SERLEENA AND BEN.....
cont'd

.....WE SEE ROOTS COME OUT OF SERLEENA'S CHEST.....
HANDS
cont'd

.....AND LIFT UP BEN AS RITA PEEKS OUT IN B/G.

.....AND COMES BACK UP TO WATCH MORE.

FROM BEHIND RITA - SERLEENA, BEN AND SCRAD IN B/G.....
cont'd

SCRAD'S POV OF EMPTY BACK ROOM.

SINGLE - SERLEENA LOOKING TO BACK ROOM.
"YOU IDIOTS SEE ANYTHING?"

.....AND THEN CHARLIE, AT THE BACK DOOR.

TWO SHOT- SCRAD AND CHARLIE AT THE BACK DOOR.

SINGLE- SERLEENA LOOKING AT BEN, WITH SCRAD AND SOMETIMES CHARLIE IN THE B/G.

OTS SERLEENA ONTO BEN.....
cont'd

.....HER ROOT COMES INTO SHOT.....
cont'd

AND RIPS HIS HEAD IN HALF

.....AND RIPS HIS HEAD IN HALF. THE SKIN FALLS OUT OF SHOT.....
cont'd

SINGLE- BEN IS SLICED IN HALF.....

.....REVEALING A SPARKLE OF LIGHT. .....
cont'd

147

JAY Nope.
SECURITY GUARD I see you neuralyzed another partner.

He gets in the elevator.

INT. MIB HALLWAY—NIGHT—MOMENTS LATER

The elevator doors open. Jay steps out. Aliens and MIB agents go about their business.

We follow Jay through MIB.

TWO MIB AGENTS, BEE AND DEE, stand next to the ALIEN. Actually Dee is standing next to the ALIEN; Bee is STANDING ON THE CEILING UPSIDE DOWN.

JAY Bee, Dee, next time you use a fission carbonizer, put a sub-molecular de-atomizer on the barrel so it doesn't sound like a cannon...
(to one of the aliens) Hey! Get some booties on them things. You're crappin' up the floor!

Jay crosses by TWO OTHER AGENTS.

JAY Check his visa. Cephalopods have been making counterfeits at the Kinko's on Canal.

AGENTS are pushing a GIANT, DEAD ALIEN through the main floor.

JAY And would somebody please explain to me why I have a dead Tricrainasloph going through Passport Control?

Jay crosses by and stops.

YOUNG AGENT That'd be my fault, sir. I'm very sorry, sir. Please don't neuralyze me, sir.
JAY What the hell is that supposed to mean?
YOUNG AGENT Nothing, sir.

Jay walks off.

INT. ZED'S OFFICE—NIGHT

ZED is at his desk. Jay enters.

ZED Good work in the subway. I remember Jeff when he was yay high.
JAY What ya got for me?
ZED Take a look out that window. See those guys in black suits? They work here, too. We've got it covered.
JAY Zed...C'mon, man, what ya got?
ZED Listen, dedication's one thing but if you let it, this job'll eat you up and spit you out whole. You wanna look like me when you hit 50?...

Jay gives him a look.

ZED ...ish.
JAY I'll be in the gym if you need me.

As Jay starts to go.

ZED All right, there was a killing earlier. 177 Spring. Alien on alien. Why don't you take Tee with you and make a report.
JAY Uhh. Tee. Uhh, right. What happened...see what happened with Tee...We, uh...

FRANK THE PUG enters. He has a folder in his mouth, which he drops in a chair.

FRANK Passports. No rush. How they hangin', Jay?
ZED You've got to stop neuralyzing MIB personnel.
JAY The dude was crying in the middle of the diner.
FRANK I hate that.
JAY And plus, you can't count Elle. I mean, she wanted to go back to the morgue...I helped her.
ZED You need a partner.
JAY I'm cool.
FRANK I'll be his partner.

Zed looks at Frank, then back to Jay.

INT. MIB IMPOUND—A SHORT TIME LATER

TRACK down a long row of identical BLACK FORD LTD'S. Jay and Frank enter shot.

Frank is wearing an MIB suit, shirt, and tie.

FRANK Jay! Wait up! I appreciate the shot, man. Thought I'd never get out of that mail room.
JAY Lose the suit.
FRANK Sure thing, partner. Just goin' for the look, but if I do say so myself, I find the overall effect very slimming. Not that I've had any problems with the ladies, or what have you. It's just that when you get down to brass tacks...

A BLACK MERCEDES-BENZ E500 lights up, pulls forward, and both doors swing open.

FRANK Whoa! Nice sled! Very swank, heated seats. Sometimes I get hives.

INT. MERCEDES—NIGHT

Jay and Frank are driving; Frank's singing "*I WILL SURVIVE.*"

JAY Frank! Bring your head in the window before I roll it up in there!

FRANK Got it.

Frank continues humming.

JAY Frank!

As they continue driving.

FRANK (o.s.) …For my money, it's missionary.…Anyway…I was in the Bowery the other night and I meet this Great Dane…a little thin in the body…but very pretty in the face.
JAY Frank, that's just not appealing to me, man. Seriously.

EXT. BEN'S FAMOUS PIZZA (OF SOHO)—NIGHT

Jay and Frank arrive.

FRANK Okay…So I'd say we do the good cop, bad cop thing. You interrogate the witness and I growl.

They get out of the car.

JAY No, wait. How about we do the good cop, dumb dog thing and you just shut up!
FRANK You got it, partner. Total silence. Absolute quiet. Not a word out of me.

INT. BEN'S FAMOUS PIZZA (OF SOHO)—NIGHT—A SHORT TIME LATER

A few AGENTS dust for fingerprints. Others scan the room with magnetic imaging devices.

Jay and Frank enter. They cross to an agent making notes.

FRANK What do we got?

Jay gives him a look. Frank "zips" his mouth and "throws" away the "key."

JAY *(to agent)* What do we got?
AGENT *(pointing to where Ben exploded)* There's a phosphorus residue on the wall and floor. We've sent samples back to M for analysis.

Frank nods to BEN'S flat, empty body.

FRANK Hey, Jay—Zero percent body fat.

The agent laughs. Jay gives him a look.

AGENT *(shrugs)* Funny.
JAY Witness?
AGENT Girl. Saw everything.

The agent hands Jay a NAPKIN. On one side is the LOGO of the

pizza parlor. *A TRIANGULAR SLICE OF PIZZA on its side. The top corner points STRAIGHT TO THE STATUE OF LIBERTY in the distance—A STAR IN THE SKY TWINKLES ABOVE LADY LIBERTY.*

The agent has scrawled the witness's name. LAURA VASQUEZ.

AGENT She's taking it pretty well.

Jay spots AGENT C in the back room interrogating Laura.

LAURA …No, you listen to me. I don't answer any more of your questions until you answer mine. I want to know what happened here.

Jay puts the napkin in his pocket.

JAY I think I'd better handle this one.
FRANK You got it.
JAY *(to Frank)* Alone. The whole talking-dog thing might be a bit much for her right now.
FRANK Whadda ya want me to do?
JAY Sniff around.

Jay exits. The agent laughs. Frank gives him a look.

FRANK What?
AGENT *(shrugs)* Funny.

BACK ROOM

Jay enters.

AGENT C Try taking a deep breath, ma'am. Everything's gonna be all right.
JAY Just what part of this is she supposed to feel all right about?

Jay motions for Agent C to leave. He does.

JAY I'm Agent Jay. Why don't you tell me exactly what you saw.
LAURA I saw a two-headed guy. And a woman in leather.
JAY Caucasian?
LAURA Grey. With tentacles that were coming out of her hands. And she used them to rip…
JAY *(cutting her off)* …the skin off his body. Actually, it's not skin. It's a proto-plasma polymer similar to the chemical makeup to the gum you find in baseball cards. What's the last thing you ate prior to the incident?
LAURA Calzone.
JAY What time?
LAURA Lunch.
JAY Spinach?
LAURA Mushroom.

He considers that.

JAY You need pie.

EXT. DINER—NIGHT—ESTABLISHING

The small, neighborhood diner.

INT. DINER—NIGHT—A SHORT TIME LATER

The same diner where Jay neuralyzed Tee. Jay and Laura are at a table eating.

LAURA …The light. They kept asking Ben about a light. Light of Zartha. Something like that.

Her hand is shaking. She puts down her fork.

JAY You okay?
LAURA An hour ago a man I've known my whole life vanished right in front of my eyes because of a woman with things coming out of her fingers and a two-headed guy with an IQ of a fire hydrant. So yeah…everything's okay.
(off Jay's look)
Look…When we were kids…before we're taught how to think or what to believe…our hearts tell us that there's something else out there. Now I know what I saw. You tell me what I'm supposed to believe.

She looks into his eyes searching for answers.

JAY I'm a member of a secret organization that polices and monitors alien activity on planet Earth. Ben was an alien and so were the people who killed him. Now I don't know why they did it but I promise you that I'm going to find out.
LAURA Okay.
JAY Okay?
LAURA Okay.
JAY Okay.

Jay takes out his neuralyzer.

JAY Look…I'm sorry. I'm gonna have to…
LAURA Kill me.
JAY No. Just a little flash and everything goes back the way it was.
LAURA After you…flash me…if I see you again, will I know it's you?
JAY I'll see you, but you won't see me.

Jay clicks a button on the neuralyzer. We hear it whine.

LAURA Must be hard. Must be very lonely.

Jay notices a bicycle with two riders go by the window. Their bicycle and bodies are surrounded by little lights. Jay's communicator beeps.

JAY Excuse me. *(retracting his neuralyzer)*
I gotta go.

LAURA What about the "flashy" thing?
JAY I'll flash you some other time.

Jay gets up and exits.

EXT. DINER/MERCEDES—NIGHT—MOMENTS LATER

Frank is listening to the radio. "I WILL SURVIVE."

Jay clicks off the radio and gets in.

FRANK What? Did you tell the girl you love her?
JAY Hey, man. She's a witness to a crime. That's it.
FRANK Yada yada. You're attracted. She's not even my species and I'm attracted.
JAY I'm supposed to take advice on love from a dude that chases his own ass?

As the car peels out.

FRANK Canine profiling, and I resent it.

SNAP CUT TO:

EXT. CENTRAL PARK—LATER THAT NIGHT

Trucks are parked next to a LITTLE YELLOW TENT. MIB agents are everywhere.

The Mercedes pulls up. Jay and Frank get out. As they cross to the little yellow tent…

FRANK Hey, Jay. Wait up. *(to the agents)* Comin' through. MIB brass. Look sharp. I'm Agent F now, Agent Jay's new partner. Who you eye-balling?…Huh.

Jay stops.

JAY Frank. Cool out, dog.

Jay crosses off. An agent laughs.

FRANK *(to agent)* Got kids?

CENTRAL PARK AGENT No.

FRANK Want 'em?

Frank shows his teeth and gives a little growl. WE HEAR O.S. screams of Frank ripping into the agent.

INT. MIB TENT—NIGHT

Jay walks toward the 18-INCH SPACECRAFT. Jay takes an endoscopic device and inserts the end with a tiny light and camera into an opening in the spacecraft. He plugs the endoscope into his communicator and sees Zed.

ZED Talk to me.

We cut back and forth.

JAY It's Kylothian. Class C.
ZED (o.s.) Serleena.

INT. MAIN HALL

JAY (o.s.) Serleena? Old girlfriend?
ZED She wishes.

Jay over the communicator screen.

JAY When it says that the perps were looking for the Light of...

PUSH IN ON: ZED

ZED Zartha.
JAY Yeah. What is it?
ZED This makes no sense. The Light's not on Earth. We took care of this a long time ago.
JAY Well, obviously not.
ZED Very bad news—Twenty-five years ago the Zarthans came to Earth trying to hide the Light from Serleena.
JAY *(over the communicator)* Well, we don't do that.
ZED That's right. That's why I ordered it off the planet. That was one war I did not want to be in the middle of.
JAY Well, Zed...I got a Kylothian Class C in the middle of my park. Are you sure this light isn't still here?
ZED Positive. I gave the order. My best agent carried it out. It's as if I gave the order to you.
JAY Well, let's just ask the agent...
ZED Can't.
JAY Dead?
ZED Sort of. He works at the post office.

A beat. The CAMERA TRACKS IN.

JAY No.

PUSH IN ON: EGG SCREEN

ZED If Serleena gets to Kay before we do...He's dead. The Earth's very existence may rest on what Kay knows—it's too bad you wiped out his entire memory of it. Bring him in. Now.

EXT. TRURO CITY POST OFFICE—MORNING—ESTABLISHING

As we follow the Mercedes to the post office.

FRANK (o.c.) You're still mad. I had to take a leak. What's the big deal?
JAY (o.c.) The big deal is...you can't just walk into a gas station and scream, "Yo! Grease monkey! Where's the little pugs' room?"

FRANK (o.c.) You expect me to pee on the sidewalk?

INT. MERCEDES—CONTINUOUS

As Jay pulls up.

JAY Stay.
FRANK Hey, listen, partner. I may look like a dog, but I only play one here on Earth.
JAY Whatever...Wipe your mouth.
FRANK *(to a passing dog)* Hey babe.

INT. TRURO POST OFFICE—DAY

Jay walks in.

KAY (o.c.) Good people of Truro, Mass., may I kindly have your attention...

Jay looks up to see Kay, behind one of the windows.

KAY In order to facilitate your shipping needs, I'd like to remind you that all packages must be properly wrapped...

He holds up a pathetically wrapped package.

...this one is an example of "go home and do it again"...I think you know what I mean, Mrs. Vigushin. Brown paper and triple twist twine are the preferred media. Thank you for your time.

Jay crosses up to the window.

JAY Kay?

Kay looks up. He points to the sign above his window.

KAY C. Express mail, two-day air.

Jay looks at Kay's name tag. KEVIN.

JAY Kevin. Kevin. That's funny, you just...you don't look like a Kevin...

Kay just stares at him.

JAY You don't remember me but we used to work together.
KAY *(re: Jay's suit)* I never worked at a funeral home.
Is there something I can do for you, slick?
JAY Okay...straight to the point. You are a former agent of a top-secret organization that monitors the extraterrestrials on Earth. We are the Men In Black. We have a situation and we need your help.
KAY There's a free mental health clinic on the corner of Lilac and East Valley. Next!

A young girl, ELIZABETH, muscles her way in.

ELIZABETH Twenty Rugrats stamps, please.
KAY Elizabeth! The United States Postal Office hasn't quite kept up with today's youth, but I can offer you some new Berlin airlift stamps.
ELIZABETH No.
KAY Opera legends?
ELIZABETH No.
KAY American Samoa?
ELIZABETH No.
KAY Amish quilts?
JAY S'cuse me, sweetie. I'm sorry...I've got a world to save here.

He lifts Elizabeth out of the way.

JAY *(then, to Kay)* There was no coma. It was all a cover.
KAY Who are you?
JAY Question is, who are you?
KAY I'm Postmaster of Truro, Massachusetts, and I am ordering you to leave the premises.

Kay crosses off.

JAY Kay!

INT. TRURO POST OFFICE/ MAIL SORTING AREA—DAY

Kay crosses in. A YOUNG POSTAL EMPLOYEE is at the coffee maker.

KAY That decaf?

The coffee pot slips from his shaking hands and falls to the floor.

YOUNG EMPLOYEE Sorry.
KAY All right people, we have a breach. Farrell, cordon off this area...Billings, I'll have a full perimeter wipe-down. Right here, right now.

Jay crosses in.

JAY Kay...
KAY Farrell, get a mop and escort all nonessential personnel from this site immediately!!
JAY Listen to yourself, Kay! Who talks like that?

Jay takes out a PALM COMPUTER DEVICE. He holds it up to the postal employees. On the display we see what planet they're from, what language they speak.

JAY Skalluch.

All the POSTAL EMPLOYEES stop what they're doing. Jay holds up his MIB ID.

JAY Hytuu saee habbilmuu.

Kay looks over at the handful of employees. THEY HAVE ALL

REVEALED THEIR VARIOUS ALIEN SELVES. Tentacles. Beaks.

JAY *(to Kay)* Why do you think you're so comfortable here? Just about everybody that works at the post office is an alien.

Jay reaches under the MACHINE that's sorting letters. He punches a code. The door swings open. A MULTI-LIMBED CREATURE is actually doing the sorting at a mind-numbing pace. One of the limbs holds a cigarette...another a Starbuck's latte. Jay closes the hatch.

Kay takes it all in. No expression. He crosses to the MULTI-LIMBED CREATURE. He grabs the cigarette—looks at the CREATURE—

KAY No smoking.

EXT. TRURO POST OFFICE—DAY—SECONDS LATER

Jay catches up to Kay as he is getting into a mail delivery jeep.

JAY Kay!
KAY The wife and I went to Las Vegas. We saw Sigfreid and Roy fly a white tiger around the room. Your act's nothing special, junior.
JAY When you look up at the stars at night, you get a feeling deep down in your gut like you don't know who you are—like you know more about what is going on out there than you do down here. It's why she left you, Kay. That's why your wife left you.

Kay's FIST goes flying directly at JAY. It lands on Jay's NOSE.

JAY *(shaking it off)* Okay, I'll tell you what...

(then) You decide you want to know who you really are, you come take a ride with me. If not, people are waiting for their *TV Guides*.

Jay walks off.

EXT. TRURO POST OFFICE—DAY—MOMENTS LATER

INSIDE MERCEDES—MOMENTS LATER

Jay gets in behind the wheel.

FRANK Think he'll bite?

After a beat, Kay slides in next to him.

KAY I'm just going for a ride. If things don't add up, it's hasta luego. You know what I mean?

Jay starts the car.

FRANK Hey, Kay.

Kay glances in the back seat. The little pug is there.

FRANK How's it hangin'?
JAY Your replacement.

EXT. MIB—DAY—ESTABLISHING

INT. MIB HEADQUARTERS—DAY

Jay, Kay, and Frank stride in on their way to the elevators.

GUARD *(not looking up from his paper)*
Good to see ya, Kay.
KAY Good to see you, too.

They get on the elevator.

KAY Whoever you are.
(then) Well, let's see what you got here, chief.

As the elevator doors close, Jay looks at Kay.

INT. MIB HEADQUARTERS—MAIN HALL—DAY

The elevator doors open. Jay steps out. Frank and Kay follow.

ALIENS of all description move about. MIB AGENTS everywhere. Kay hears his name whispered. Several MIB AGENTS actually give him a respectful nod and salute.

MIB AGENT №1 Welcome back, Agent Kay.
MIB AGENT №2 Agent Kay...

Kay takes it all in as they continue through the main hall. ROOKIE AGENT GEE catches up to them.

GEE Don't mean to bother you, Agent Jay, but...
(spots Kay) Oh-my-God. You're Agent Kay!
KAY That's what they tell me.

Gee eases Jay out of the way to get closer to Kay.

GEE This really is an honor. Gee. Agent Gee.
(then, to Jay) The legend. Most respected agent in the history of MIB. The most feared human in the universe. In the flesh.
(to Kay) Maybe I could buy you a cup of coffee sometime. Hear some of the old war stories.
KAY Black, with two sugars if you're going.
GEE An honor.
JAY I'll take a...My man!

But Gee is already gone.

INT. MIB HEADQUARTERS—NIGHT

Zed is at the egg screen.

ZED How'd it go?

Reveal MICHAEL JACKSON on the egg screen. He's dressed in a BLACK SUIT. He's in the ANTARCTIC, standing on a glacier, shivering from the cold.

MICHAEL Zed, the Drolacks are gone and the treaty is signed.
ZED Good work.
MICHAEL Zed, what about that position you promised me in Men in Black?
ZED Still working on the Alien Affirmative Action program. I'll keep you posted.
MICHAEL Wait a minute. That's not what you promised me...
ZED Y- You're breaking up.
MICHAEL Zed...Hello...? I can be Agent M.
ZED I can't hear you. I'll call you back...

Zed SHUTS Michael OFF, then turns to see Jay, Kay, and Frank.

ZED Kay!

Zed gives him a friendly slap on the back.

ZED I think Earth might be in a bad way and you may be the only one who can save it.
KAY Well, you know, neither rain nor snow.
ZED Good man. Get him armed and up to speed and then over to Deneuralyzation.

They exit. As Frank is about to follow them out...

ZED Frank. Frank, I'm gonna need them together on this one.

Frank hangs his head.

FRANK Ouch.
ZED I'm looking for a new assistant.

Frank looks back up.

ZED It's not field work, but you get better dental.
FRANK Dental?

Frank smiles, revealing HORRIBLE PUG TEETH.

INT. TECH UNIT—OFF MAIN HALL—CONTINUOUS

Jay and Kay enter. The room is filled with strange, fascinating machines and technologies.

JAY This is the Tech Unit. The most advanced technologies from all over the universe are in this room.

Kay moves to a machine with a GLOWING HOLOGRAPHIC GLOBE at its center.

KAY What's this?

He pokes his finger in the holographic OCEAN creating a tiny, little ripple. Jay looks over, not paying attention...

EXT. JARITHIA 5

Fifty million light years away. A HUGE FINGER comes out of their sky and dips into their ocean. ALIEN CREATURES of the actual planet run as a GIANT TIDAL WAVE throws a massive shadow over their entire city. ONE ALIEN runs toward camera shrieking...

JARITHIAN *(subtitled)* All is lost! All is lost!

INT. TECH UNIT—OFF MAIN HALL—CONTINUOUS

Kay inspects the globe.

JAY Don't touch that!
KAY I didn't do anything.
JAY Hands in your pockets.

Jay opens a metal cabinet, reaches in and grabs the intimidating SERIES 4 DE-ATOMIZER.

JAY Your favorite weapon...
KAY That?
JAY Yeah. Let's go put it on.
KAY What?
JAY The last suit you'll ever wear. Again.

INT. DENEURALYZER ROOM—AT THE SAME TIME

Jay enters, then Kay. Kay is wearing his MIB SUIT. They stand side-by-side. Jay points to the strange machine.

JAY The deneuralyzer. In a few moments transverse magneto energy will surge through your brain, unlocking information hidden deep and dormant that could hold the key to the Earth's very survival.
KAY *(points)* Okay. What's that thing?
JAY The deneuralyzer.

INT. MIB CUSTOMS AREA—DAY—AT THE SAME TIME

TRACK DOWN a line of IMMIGRANTS waiting in line for processing. WE SETTLE on a FEMALE FIGURE who steps up to an AGENT.

MIB CUSTOMS AGENT Name and planet of origin?

Serleena looks up.

SERLEENA Serleena Xath. Planet Jorn. Kyloth System.
MIB CUSTOMS AGENT Any fruits or vegetables?

She points to Scrad and Charlie.

SERLEENA Yes. Two heads of cabbage.
MIB CUSTOMS AGENT Reason for visit?
SERLEENA Education. I really want to learn how to be an underwear model.

The AGENT looks up.

SERLEENA They told me I've got real potential.

She opens her coat. VICTORIA'S SECRET UNDERWEAR. AGENTS LOOK UP.

Scrad and Charlie fall to the floor. Scrad's eyes roll up in his head.

CHARLIE Help! Heart attack!

Charlie begins CPR.

CHARLIE Wake up, champ!

He blows breaths into Scrad's mouth and pounds on his own chest.

Other MIB AGENTS run over to assist. The diversion gives Serleena enough time to pick off both groups of agents with neural roots coming out of either hand.

The NEURAL ROOTS turn on each other, multiplying and entangling the agents, trapping them in an ever-growing mass of brambles...

INT. MAIN HALLWAY—LAB ROOM—MOMENTS LATER

We see the FEET, HANDS, and HEADS of various MIB AGENTS poking out of the intricate mass of NEURAL ROOT BRAMBLE that now fills part of the room.

Charlie nods, turns to Scrad.

They follow her out. We settle on the DEAD ALIEN.

FRANK *(from inside the alien)* Ah jeez.

INT. DENEURALYZER ROOM—DAY—CONTINUOUS

SIREN. The glass door slams shut, sealing off the glass room. PUSH IN: ON JAY.

JAY Breach.

As Jay helps Kay out of the deneuralyzer.

JAY Breach. We're being fire-walled and flushed.
They are standing in the middle of a room that looks like a LARGE GLASS BOWL.
KAY Flushed?
JAY You ever been to a water park?
KAY I don't know.

A DRAIN appears in THE FLOOR beneath them. BLUE WATER rushes in...they are hurled around the bowl twice...and literally FLUSHED OUT. THE FLOOR reappears.

INT. DARK TUNNEL—DAY—CONTINUOUS

A length of enclosed glass pipe. We hear MUFFLED SCREAMS, which get louder as Jay and Kay hurtle by in the glass plumbing tube.

INSIDE THE GLASS PIPE

Bodies bank, turn, and corkscrew.

CLOSE—KAY

His face pulled back from the G-force.

CLOSE—JAY

His face pulled back from the G-force.

WHOOSH.

EXT. TIMES SQUARE—DUSK

TWO LARGE TANKS MARKED NITROGEN on the corner of 42nd and Broadway. A door opens revealing Jay and Kay, side by side, in their own tanks, soaking wet.

PEDESTRIANS rush past, never giving the two of them a second glance.

JAY …fyyyyy!!!
(beat)
Flushed. Yeah, man, back when you were an agent, you used to love getting flushed. Yeah, every Saturday night, you'd be like, "Flush me, Jay, flush me." I'd be like, "No!"
(then)
You can't quit on me now, Kay.

KAY I save the world and you tell me why I stare at the stars.
JAY Sure…okay.

Jay hits a button on the car alarm hanging from his key chain.

JAY Hop in.
KAY Hop in what?

The Mercedes-Benz screams around a corner and squeals to a stop in front of them…an MIB AGENT behind the wheel. Jay hits another button and the INFLATABLE AGENT is sucked into the steering wheel's air-bag compartment.

KAY Does that come standard?
JAY Actually it came with a black dude, but he kept getting pulled over.

INT. MAIN HALLWAY—LAB ROOM

Serleena, filing her nails, is walking with Scrad and Charlie.

SERLEENA Silly little planet. You could rule the place with the right set of mammary glands.

INT. MERCEDES-BENZ—CONTINUOUS

Jay speaks into his communicator.

JAY Computer. Surveillance. MIB.

A ROTATING SERIES OF IMAGES within MIB. We see the aftermath of the takeover.

JAY MIB's locked down.

Something catches his eye.

JAY Computer. Magnify—times ten. Communicator, Frank.

The monitor in the AUTOPSY ROOM. He hits the button for his CAR COMMUNICATOR.

INT. MIB HEADQUARTERS—MAIN ROOM—CONTINUOUS

The DEAD ALIEN. We hear a TONE.

Frank pops up out of the dead guts. He's got a headset on.

FRANK Jay? Where are you, partner?

Cut back and forth.

JAY We got flushed.
FRANK MIB's Code 101.
JAY Yeah, who did it?

Frank peers over the dead alien corpse to see Serleena.

FRANK Some chick in leather. I think I've seen her in a Victoria's Secret catalog.
JAY Stay where you are. I'll keep in touch.
FRANK Yeah, stay where I am.

CLICK.

Frank disappears in the dead alien.

FRANK (o.c.) Idiots…

INT. MIB—AT THE SAME TIME

Scrad/Charlie following after Serleena.

SERLEENA Have you found Kay?
SCRAD Neuralyzed.
CHARLIE Not active. Civilian.
SERLEENA What?!

Quickly back and forth.

SCRAD But he was…

CHARLIE ...here.
SCRAD To get...
CHARLIE ...deneuralyzed.
SERLEENA Deneuralyzed?
SCRAD Memory's shot. Erased. We'll find him.
CHARLIE Don't put anything in our ears.
SCRAD (O.S.) What?

Serleena walks off. Scrad/Charlie follows.

INT. MERCEDES—CONTINUOUS

Kay is looking at something.

KAY What do you make of that? I found it in the pocket of my coat.

He hands Jay a photograph.

CLOSE—PHOTOGRAPH

A YOUNGER KAY, POINTING AND SMILING. The background is slightly off.

KAY Weird, huh?
JAY Yeah, you're smiling.
KAY Is that deneuralyzer thing the only one?
JAY Only official one. Plans leaked out on the Internet a few years ago. Computer. Internet. Deneuralyzer.

WEB BROWSER START PAGE COMES UP.

Jay hits another button from the steering wheel.

eBay WEB SITE. Jay types in DENEURALYZER.

The eBay page is up. FOUND 1 OF 1 ITEMS: "DENEURALYZER."

Click. NEVER USED. BIDS START AT $200,000. WOULD CONSIDER TRADE FOR BMW Z8.

Jay scrolls down. SELLER: JACKJEEBS@...

JAY Perfect. It's an old friend.

KAY That computer is really interesting. Do I know how to use one of these?

EXT. JEEBS'S PAWN SHOP—NIGHT

Jay and Kay arrive and get out of the car.

JAY (to Kay) Why don't you just lay here and let me go...
KAY (pointing) I'll lay here.

INT. JEEBS'S PAWN SHOP—NIGHT

Jeebs turns as Jay enters.

JEEBS Hey, Jay! I ain't seen you in a while. Yo, did you see that drop top thing out front? Oh, yeah, my business is banging...You gotta check out the Web Site. Jeebsy dot...
(stops, sees Kay)
Okay, what? He's retired, right?
JAY We need the deneuralyzer.
Jeebs looks at Kay.
JEEBS You're kidding.
JAY The meter's running, Jeebs.

Jeebs leans over the counter toward Kay.

JEEBS Do you remember me?
KAY Can't say I do. I'm pretty good with faces.
(pointing to Jeebs's nose)
I think I'd remember that.
JEEBS HA! The great Kay's a neutral.

Kay gets in his face.

KAY You're standin' between me and my memories, pal. Do you have this deneuralyzer thing or not?
JEEBS No. Fresh out. Can't help you. Don't got it.

Jeebs looks from Kay to Jay. Jay gives him a look.

JEEBS Even if I did—if this doesn't work, he dies, you blow my head off. If it does work, I've brought back Kay, who just for the fun of it, blows my head off. So what's my incentive?

Jay has his weapon pointed directly at Jeebs's forehead.

JEEBS Okay, homey, okay. I keep it downstairs next to the snow-blowers.

INT. MIB—AT THE SAME TIME

CAMERA PANS down a line of ALIEN PRISONERS. Serleena walks the line.

SERLEENA Prisoners of MIB. The scum of the universe. Well now, it's the scum's turn. See, I'm in a bit of a jam, so I'm gonna make this simple. I need the Light of Zartha and Kay knows where it is. So...Whoever brings Kay to me gets Earth.

Serleena turns to Scrad/Charlie.

SERLEENA Start by finding a deneuralyzer. They're gonna want to get his memory back.
CHARLIE Check.

As Scrad/Charlie crosses out.

SERLEENA And if you fail—I'll kill you and I'll make you watch...
(to the aliens)
Now.

They file out.

INT. JEEBS'S BASEMENT—SHORT TIME LATER

Kay is seated in the deneuralyzer. Exposed wire. Part of an I-MAC computer. Gaffer's tape. A plumbing pipe here and there...it basically resembles an electric chair.

JEEBS Okay, that should do it. Now if I could have your attention for a brief moment while we go over the safety procedures. Keep your hands and feet inside the vehicle at all times and if at any point during the ride you become disoriented, there's nothing we can do about it.

Jeebs shoves a mouthpiece in Kay's mouth.

JEEBS Have you removed all jewelry?

Jay becomes frustrated.

JEEBS Are you allergic to shellfish?
JAY Jeebs!
JEEBS Right then. Smoke 'em if you got 'em.
JAY Have you ever used this thing before?
JEEBS I used the exhaust once to make some hot air popcorn, but that's about it.

Kay stares at Jeebs.

JEEBS Okay. Let's make it happen, cap'n.

Jeebs hits a switch and the deneuralyzer is activated.

EXT. NEW YORK CITY—NIGHT

All over the city HUGE POWER SURGES.

INT. JEEBS'S BASEMENT—NIGHT

BACK TO KAY

Only an instant has passed.

Jeebs turns the switch off. Kay launches backwards onto the floor. He shakes uncontrollably as smoke pours out of his ears. Then still. DEAD STILL.

JEEBS Perfect!

TWO SHOT: Jay and Jeebs lean in.

Jeebs's head EXPLODES off his body, right next to Jay, who doesn't flinch.

Kay is holding the NOISY CRICKET.

JAY You're back?
KAY No.
JAY Then how'd you know his head would grow back?
KAY It grows back?

Jeebs's head starts reforming.

JEEBS Real nice. Okay, that's the last time that I help out a friend.
JAY Kay, do you remember anything?
KAY Good-bye.

Kay crosses up the stairs.

JAY Kay...
JEEBS Kay, wait! I never got the updated software. I'm still working off of the 6.0. Your brain needs to re-boot! Give it a minute!
JAY Kay!

Kay's gone.

JEEBS From the bottom of my heart, Jay—I'm really sorry. I hope this doesn't affect our friendship—all those years of loyalty and trust, and respect for one another.

CRACK. The back wall is kicked in.

Jay tumbles out of sight behind the DENEURALYZER.

FOUR ARMED ALIENS enter.

JEEBS *(pointing)* Right over there.

ALIEN #1 shoots the DENEURALYZER. BOOM. It disintegrates...revealing Jay...who has his weapon trained on the ALIENS. The ALIENS have their weapons pointed at him. They circle each other in a Mexican standoff.

ALIEN №1 Where's Kay?
JEEBS He's not here.

Jeebs is about to speak again. Jay BLOWS HIS HEAD OFF. Jeebs staggers out of the room.

JAY Kay is officially retired. I'm his trigger-happy replacement. Something I can do for you gentlemen?
JEEBS Oh great. Right in the pie hole. Now nothing's gonna taste right.

The standoff continues.

ALIEN №2 Lower weapon.
JAY No.

TWO ALIEN ARMS burst through the wall behind Jay. One arm wraps around his throat. The other arm jerks Jay's weapon out of his hand...

The ALIEN tosses Jay across the room. ALIEN #2 catches him with a forearm to the throat in midair.

Jay lands sprawled on the floor...at the feet of SCRAD/CHARLIE.

SCRAD Jay...How are you, Boo Boo. Look, these guys really need Kay.
JAY He's neutral.
SCRAD Yeah, tell me something we don't know.
CHARLIE Yeah, tell me something we don't...

Charlie SNEEZES across the back of Scrad's head. Scrad just stares straight ahead.

CHARLIE I am sooo sorry.
ALIEN №2 God bless you.
CHARLIE Thank you.
SCRAD Look, if I don't bring Kay back to MIB, Serleena's gonna kick *my* ass. Where is he?
JAY Where's who?

Alien #1 leans in.

ALIEN №1 You don't look too good.

Jay hits him in the face, exposing his grisly face.

JAY And you look like crap.

Alien #2 laughs.

JAY I'll take that back. He looks like crap.

Alien #2 laughs and Alien #3 looks at him.

ALIEN №2 Bend him.
SCRAD Bend him.
JAY Bend him? Aw, wait, man. Nah, don't bend him.

ALIEN #1 picks Jay up...lifts him over his head...and bends his spine back...

...till it looks like it might break.

JAY AHHHHHH...

CUT TO:

EXT. JEEBS'S PAWN SHOP—NIGHT—AT THE SAME TIME

Kay steps back out onto the curb. As he waits to cross, he looks around.

Something catches his eye...

THE TWO-PERSON BICYCLE WITH BLINKING LIGHTS glides by, boom box thumping. A STREET PERSON pushes a grocery cart filled with junk. Kay looks at the cart as it passes. TWO GLOWING RED EYES. Little ALIEN HANDS peek out of the cart.

A POSTMAN walks by. Kay sees him tuck A SCALY TAIL back in his shorts.

Kay starts to go, then looks down at the sidewalk. Next to his shoe is a COCKROACH. He lifts his shoe to squish it, then stops.

EXT. JEEBS'S PAWN SHOP—NIGHT

Back to Kay. He looks at the cockroach.

His shoe comes down gently next to it. The cockroach looks up.

COCKROACH Damn decent of you.
KAY Don't mention it.

The cockroach scurries off.

WE PUSH IN ON: Kay. He looks up at the night sky. A slight smile crosses his face.

INT. JEEBS'S BASEMENT—CONTINUOUS

Jay is still above ALIEN #1, being bent backwards. He sweats and shakes trying to will away the pain.

Charlie lowers his head.

CHARLIE I think I'm gonna be sick.
SCRAD You don't wanna do that.
(beat)
Fellas, you know what? I think he's telling the truth.
ALIEN №1 Then he's no good to us.

Jay goes limp. ALIEN #1 throws him to the floor.

SHARK-MOUTH ALIEN is about to blow Jay away with his gun when...BOOM! HE VAPORIZES.

WHIP PAN TO: KAY...holding the Noisy Cricket.

KAY Didn't I teach you anything, kid?
JAY Pineal eye.

The ALIENS RUSH KAY.

Kay grabs the cap off ALIEN #3's head, exposing a single eye. He nails it with his fist.

JAY Kay, the Ballchinion.

Kay pulls on ALIEN #4's shirt and exposes TWO FLESH BALLS hanging from either side of his face.

He roundhouses the balls.

JAY (pointing) Go for the mosh tendrils!

Kay rips tendrils from the mosh tendrils's chin and he goes flying through the ceiling.

KAY Looks like you were in a pretty tight spot, kid.
JAY I had this one handled.
KAY You need a partner.
JAY I had one. Job got too tough for him.
KAY I'm back. You got some dust on your coat.
JAY So you got your memory back?
KAY Yeah.
JAY Why did Serleena take over MIB?
KAY Don't know.
JAY Cool. What is the Light of Zartha?
KAY Never heard of it.
JAY Okay.

As they go upstairs, the CAMERA BOOMS DOWN to reveal Scrad/Charlie hidden in a pile of Jeebs's junk.

SCRAD We got problems.
CHARLIE From the day we were born.

EXT. JEEBS'S—NIGHT

Jay and Kay exit and head for the Mercedes.

JAY If your memory's back, how come you don't remember the Light of Zartha?
KAY Must've neuralyzed myself in order to keep the information from myself.
JAY Ah. Good plan.

They both reach for the driver's door.

JAY Hey, man, what you doing?
KAY I always do the driving, right?
JAY Wait, no.
KAY I remember that.
JAY Wait, no. What you remember is you used to drive that old busted joint, see. I drive the new hotness.
(re: Kay)
Old and busted.
(re: himself)
New hotness.

Jay just stands there. Kay looks at him.

JAY Okay, here you go.

Jay hands him the keys.

JAY (o.s.) Old busted, hotness.

INT. ZED'S OFFICE—AT THE SAME TIME

CLOSE UP of Zed hanging upside down.

ZED Serleena, please!
SERLEENA (o.s.) Been a long time, Zed.

Pull back to reveal he's hanging from the ceiling.

SERLEENA I'm just touched you remembered me. Makes me fuzzy all over.
ZED Never forget a pretty...whatever you are.

She releases him and he drops to the floor.

SERLEENA (kicking him) Zed! Zed!

He comes to.

SERLEENA Look at you. Twenty-five years and you're still just such a looker.
ZED Cut out the meat and dairy. And look at you. Still a pile of squirmy crap in a different wrapper.
SERLEENA Oh, so feisty. Look, Zed, we both need the same thing.

She tosses him into his chair and hands him his communicator.

SERLEENA Bring him in.
ZED Don't think so.
SERLEENA Have we forgotten the little secret of the Light?
ZED The fail-safe device.
SERLEENA If it's not back on Zartha when it's supposed to be, Earth goes too-da-loo. I lose, you lose. I win, everything keeps spinning.
ZED All right, Serleena. You win.

Zed punches up numbers on his communicator. Hands it to Serleena.

PHONE RECORDING The Waverly Cinema is proud to present the one-thousandth showing of The Rocky Horror Picture Sh...

Zed has reached behind him and grabbed a lamp off his desk. He whacks Serleena on the side of her head.

Zed breaks free, doing THREE BACK FLIPS.

He jumps up and delivers a lethal-looking ROUNDHOUSE KICK TO SERLEENA'S HEAD...which doesn't even knock her off balance.

She swats him and he drops to the floor.

SERLEENA So feisty.

She kicks him in the head. Out cold.

Serleena looks to the MAIN HALL below. Something catches her eye.

SERLEENA'S POV:

MOVEMENT in the DEAD ALIEN below.

EXT. BEN'S FAMOUS PIZZA (OF SOHO)—NIGHT

As the Mercedes pulls up.

JAY (v.o.) ...Listen, Kay. We're wasting time. I want my headquarters back.

KAY (v.O.) Serleena took over MIB looking for me. They must think I know where the Light is. Let's see if it'll open up any clues.

JAY We got an eyewitness. You can talk to her.

KAY Things have changed. We used to neuralyze all the witnesses.

JAY See, I'd...um...originally I'd...um...No, I was going to...
(finally)
I interrogated her...

KAY Then you neuralyzed her.

JAY What do you mean?

INT. BEN'S FAMOUS PIZZA (OF SOHO)—NIGHT—CONTINUOUS

The place is empty and dark. Jay and Kay enter.

KAY What I mean is MIB Procedural Code #773/I-1, clearly states that all the personnel...

Kay ducks.

KAY Drop that weapon! No!

WHACK. Jay gets hit in the face with a pizza tray. He goes down. Kay points his Noisy Cricket at Laura. Laura holds the pizza tray.

JAY No!

Jay yanks Kay's arm down.

LAURA Oh, Jay!...I'm sorry.

JAY No, I'm fine. It's my fault. I probably...
(re: Kay)
Kay, my partner.
(re: Laura)
Laura, the witness.

KAY *(holds out his hand)* Pleasure.

LAURA Jay, thanks for sending those agents over to keep an eye on me last night. That was really sweet.

KAY MIB Procedural Code #594-B states that MIB personnel shall never be used for any other purpose...

JAY Ben—the Zarthan—was vaporized here, so I'm assuming that the perp was over here in this direction...

Kay looks like he's staring into space...

KAY Was he about five-seven? Portly fella? Thinning hair?

LAURA You knew him?

KAY Nope. Never seen him before in my life.

Kay crosses to a framed photograph on the wall.

PUSH IN ON: PHOTOGRAPH

Old photograph of Ben hanging on the wall. Ben is standing on a Montauk pier with his arm around a BASS he just caught. The background seems a little off.

KAY That...
(points to photo)
...is a helluva fish.

Jay takes out the picture Kay found in his suit. He places it on the picture of Ben. Both backgrounds line up perfectly and BEN NOW HAS HIS ARM AROUND KAY, POINTING AND LAUGHING.

JAY Helluva fish.

Jay stands to the side of the photograph trying to determine the angle Kay is pointing.

JAY You left yourself clues?

KAY Yeah, in case I had to be deneuralyzed because my replacement couldn't handle the situation.

JAY Well, if the joker that got deneuralyzed hadn't created the situation in the first place...

LAURA Boys...

They give each other a long look, then...

JAY You're pointing at something.
(to Kay)
Excuse me....The astronaut.

Jay crosses to the framed photo of an astronaut.

KAY Jay...

JAY Okay, all right, now he's pointing...He's like...
(walks to the pizza boxes)
Who stacks pizza boxes like this? Now to the layman—this is a slice of pizza, but to the trained eye this is probably Zarthan language—it means arrow...

CLOSE—KEY

Engraved on the key: GCT.

KAY Jay...!

Jay strides confidently over to a cabinet.

JAY Slowing me down, slick. Whatever we're looking for is in these cabinets, right here.

He throws the cabinet doors open and reaches in.

JAY *(displays can)* Anchovy fillets in virgin olive oil.

Kay points to A KEY hanging on the wall next to the photograph.

He takes the key off the wall.

KAY I hope I'm not slowing you down.
JAY Good work, partner. Yeah. Now we gotta figure out where it goes.
KAY I know where it goes.

Kay puts his neuralyzer in front of Laura.

JAY No. Not yet.
KAY MIB Procedural Code #773 clearly states...
JAY I know the code, Kay. But, no, she might be important to me...but to us...Well, for help...to help us later.
KAY Well, she can't stay here. They'll be back.

Kay exits.

JAY You can stay with some friends of mine.
LAURA People like you?
JAY Kinda.

SMASH CUT TO:

INT. WORM GUYS' BACHELOR PAD—NIGHT

CLOSE—THE WORM GUYS

WORM GUYS JAY!! What's going on, man? What's up. How's it going?

One WORM GUY is stretched out on the sofa reading Travel and Leisure. *Another W.G. is lifting weights. One is watching a ball game on TV next to another in a hot tub.*

JAY Hey, what's happening, fellas. MIB is Code 101.
WORMS 101! Taken over. Bad. Very bad.
JAY Listen, I need your help.

Jay grabs Laura, who is standing behind him.

JAY This is Laura.
WORMS LAU-RA. Hey, Laura. Yeah, baby.
JAY Easy, easy.
LAURA They're worms.
WORMS Once you go worm that's what you'll yearn.
JAY Yeah, that's what they say.
LAURA I've dated worse.

JAY They're under suspension right now for stealing from the duty-free shop.

WORM GEEBLE slides a huge case of cigarettes behind him on the counter.

WORM GEEBLE We were framed!
WORM SLEEBLE Zed's wormaphobic!

They go berserk and high-five each other as Kay enters.

WORMS Kay!! You're back.
SLEEBLE Somebody said you were dead. You look good!
KAY We're double-parked.

As Kay crosses out.

JAY *(to Kay)* Yeah.
(to worms)
Laura's very important to me...
(to Kay)
To us...

Kay looks over his shoulder.

JAY ...to the stuff...me and you, man, to the stuff we're doing.
(to the worms)
...Man, you got to keep an eye on her for me.
WORMS Definitely. Nooo problem. Keep both of them on her.

TV WORM motions to Laura.

TV WORM Why don't you sit right here?
WEIGHT LIFTER Oh yeah, like you gotta shot.
TV WORM Shut up.
WEIGHT LIFTER Make me.

Jay gives Laura his communicator.

JAY My communicator, in case you need it.

Laura gives Jay a KISS. A surprise to both of them. A nice surprise.

JAY Okay, just watch out for Neeble.
LAURA Which one's Neeble?
JAY Which one of you are Neeble?
NEEBLE Yo, mama!
JAY Ah, him...right there. It's fine. Everything's straight, it's safe. Don't fall asleep.

Jay runs out. Laura looks around in a slight daze. One of the WORMS holds up a BOARD GAME SPINNER.

ALL THE WORMS TWISTER!

INT. GRAND CENTRAL TERMINAL—SHORT TIME LATER

PUSH IN ON: LOCKER C17.

JAY You left yourself clues in a locker in Grand Central Station...
KAY You're not gonna slow me down on this, are you?
JAY Slow you down? Whose brain's working on outdated software?
KAY Why don't you go grab us some coffee while I do this?

Jay looks behind him.

JAY Oh, sure thing. How do you take it? Black...couple cubes of kiss my ass?
KAY I don't know what's in there. I don't want you to get hurt. So step back.
JAY Kay, for real, man. Open the damn locker.

Kay puts in the key and opens it.

EXT. TOWN INSIDE THE LOCKER—NIGHT

AN INCREDIBLE WORLD WITH TINY ALIEN INHABITANTS. They squint up as the light washes in from outside. They see Kay step into the light.

TINY ALIENS KAY! He's back! THE LIFE GIVER! All hail, Kay! All hail, Kay!

They break out into their version of "THE STAR SPANGLED BAN-NER."

JAY You the Man Who Would Be King of the Train Locker?

He gestures to a CLOCK TOWER. On the top is an old '70s- style PULSAR WITH GLOWING DIGITAL NUMBERS.

KAY Been looking everywhere for that watch.

Kay grabs the watch.

ALIENS Oh Merciful One! The clock tower! No, no...
JAY I got ya. It's cool. It's cool.

Jay puts his watch on the clock tower.

JAY Here, check this out. Titanium case. Waterproof to over 300 meters. That's banging, right?
ALIEN 1 Who are you, stranger?
JAY Jay.
ALIENS All hail Jay! All hail Jay! All hail Jay!

Jay smiles.

JAY Oh, merciful Jay. The keeper of...

Kay pulls Jay away and closes the locker. We hear the VOICE OF AN ELDER in the distance.

ELDER ALIEN (o.c.) Wait! The commandments.
ALIEN The tablet!
ALIENS The tablet! The tablet! The tablet!
ELDER ALIEN We have lived by its word and peace has reigned throughout our world...

Jay and Kay lean in.

THE CAMERA TRACKS through this fantastic ALIEN WORLD...to the ALIEN ELDER...standing on a MOUNTAINTOP. Long white beard. Robe.

HE HOLDS OUT THE TABLET.

ELDER Pass it on to others so that they too may be enlightened.

Kay reaches in. When his fingers touch it, THE CROWD CHEERS.

He pulls it out of the locker. He and Jay look at it.

CLOSE—AN OLD TAPEWORM VIDEO RENTAL CARD

with Kay's name on it. All the normal instructions and policies of the store are printed on the card—which the ALIENS BEGIN RECITING.

ALIENS Be kind, rewind!
ELDER ALIEN Go back and reconcile your past in order to move tranquilly into your future.
ALIENS Two for one every Wednesday!
ELDER ALIEN Give twice as much as ye receive on the most sacred of days—every Wednesday.
ALIEN Large adult entertainment section in the back!

THE ELDER dramatically points to the back of the locker and THE CROWD OF ALIENS ERUPT INTO HUGE CHEERS.

ANGLE ON: *Jay and Kay as the cheers continue.*

JAY That's just nasty!

Jay closes the locker door.

INT. GRAND CENTRAL HALLWAY—NIGHT

We pick up Jay and Kay as they round a corner.

JAY What's up with the video card?
KAY I don't know.
JAY Why did you leave the watch?
KAY To remind me.
JAY Of what?
KAY Can't remember.
JAY Guess.

He holds out the digital watch for Jay to see.

.....LOCKER DOOR HINGES OPEN, REVEALING J&K's FACES,....

cont'd

8 SHOT- ALIENS

OVER ALIEN #1 ONTO K

.....LEANING IN FOR A LOOK.

SINGLE ALIEN- " DID YOU BRING US FOOD? "

CONT'D

cont'd

..... MEDIUM WIDE SHOT.

REVERSE- SLOWLY THE LIGHT CUTS A PATH ACROSS
THE LOCKER.....

cont'd

cont'd

PAST CAMERA

J&K's P.O.V.- WIDE SHOT OF ELDER COMING DOWN HILL.

.....REVEALING LOCKER TOWN.....

cont'd

INSERT WATCH TOWER- K REACHES IN.....

CLOSER IN ON ELDER

.....COMPLETELY.

cont'd

.....AND TAKES THE WATCH OFF OF THE WATCH TOWER.

POP IN C/U ON ELDER

100 SHOT- ALIENS BOWING AND CHANTING. SLIGHTLY HIGH P.O.V.

SINGLE ALIEN #1- RE: WATCH

ANGLE ON RED LIGHT DISTRICT- BLINKING LIGHTS, THE WHOLE SEX THING.

CLOSE—WATCH

> 59:37

And counting down the seconds. 36,35,34...

KAY I'm guessing we have 59 minutes and 37 seconds to figure it out.

EXT. TAPEWORM VIDEO—NIGHT

The Mercedes pulls up to the store.

INT. TAPEWORM VIDEO—NIGHT—CONTINUOUS

TRACK through the video store. Instead of the normal sections...Comedy, Action, Drama...the signs read:
> *SCI-FACT AND OLIVER STONE FILMS,*
> *THE OCCULT AND OLIVER STONE FILMS,*
> *THE BIZARRE AND OLIVER STONE FILMS,*
> *CONSPIRACY AND OLIVER STONE MOVIES.*

JAY Look, so here's an idea. How about we stop chasing all these butt backwards clues, go get a couple fission carbonizers and get our headquarters back?

KAY It's all about to make sense, kid.

HAILEY, a pierced and tattooed girl in her twenties, stares vacantly at her computer screen. Kay hands her his card.

KAY Is this card valid?

HAILEY This card hasn't been used in years. Before I was born.

ANGLE ON: Jay and Kay standing at the counter.

KAY I've been away on business.

JAY Millions of frequent flyer miles.

HAILEY Try and use 'em. I always wanted to go to Cambodia. You can get a lobster dinner there for like a dollar. And the airlines said they black out holidays, you have to stay over a weekend. It's a conspiracy, I'm sure. Why would...

JAY Can you tell us anything about the account?

HAILEY Only that you never checked out a tape.

She hands Kay the card. As they start to go...

HAILEY You reserved one once, but you never picked it up.

Jay and Kay exchange looks.

HAILEY Hey, Newton!

NEWTON, a weird guy in his thirties, comes out of the back.

NEWTON There's a huge rat in the toilet. It's all stopped up, so you're gonna have to pee in the sink.

He sees Jay and Kay. Hailey points to the computer screen.

NEWTON Still think I'm paranoid?

HAILEY Yeah.

Turns to Jay and Kay.

NEWTON Gentlemen, my name's Newton. I run the place.
(leans in) Seen any aliens lately?

KAY You need professional help, son.

HAILEY He's getting it. It's not working.

NEWTON You don't recognize me? May 29th, 1996.
(off Kay's blank stare)
The city morgue? I was the guy who was slimed up on the ceiling.

KAY Oh, yeah.

NEWTON New case, huh? Light of Zartha? Got it.

PUSH IN ON: Jay and Kay

EXT. MIB HEADQUARTERS—ESTABLISHING—NIGHT

INT. MIB—NIGHT

SERLEENA Jarra. Good to see you. It's just a sin that they've kept a genius like you locked away.

JARRA Their Eagle Scout, Agent Jay, caught me siphoning the Earth's ozone to sell on the black market. They're very touchy about this global warming thing.

SERLEENA Look, I need a spacecraft. Something that can travel 300 times the speed of light. Do it, I'll give you whatever you want.

JARRA Give me Jay, we'll call it even.

SERLEENA Groovy.

Serleena nods. Jarra exits. Serleena looks over at a LITTLE ALIEN ROBOT.

SERLEENA Gatbot, got a little something special for you.

The LITTLE ROBOT follows Serleena.

INT. NEWTON'S BEDROOM—NIGHT—SHORT TIME LATER

Newton, Hailey, Jay, and Kay enter.

WOMAN (o.c.) Newton, is that you?

NEWTON Yes, Mom. I'm up here with some friends.

HAILEY I wanna have your baby.

WOMAN (o.c.) Would you like some mini-pizzas?

Newton looks to Jay and Kay.

NEWTON You guys want some mini-pizzas?

They just stare at him.

NEWTON They're good. They're like bagels with pizza stuff on 'em. She'll put a little fontina cheese on. She has palsy so she ends up putting a lot of cheese on.

They continue to stare at him.

NEWTON *(calling to mom)* No, thanks, we're cool.
(then) Over here.

They cross through the bedroom, which is filled with UFO clippings, alien artifacts, model spaceships, etc.

Newton starts going through hundreds of videotapes…incredibly organized, cross-referenced, and labeled.

NEWTON This is it.

He hands an old VIDEOTAPE to Jay. The title reads: "THE MYSTERY OF THE LIGHT OF ZARTHA." Narrated by PETER GRAVES.

JAY Finally, some hard evidence.
NEWTON Yes, gentlemen. Before I play the tape, one question: What's up with anal probing. I mean, is that really necessary? Is that something you guys…
JAY Boy! Move!
NEWTON Okay.

He shoves the tape in the VCR.

TELEVISION SCREEN:

INT. CHEESY LOW-BUDGET SET

PETER GRAVES walks out, sits on the edge of a desk and looks into camera.

PETER GRAVES Although no one has ever been able to prove their existence…a quasi-government agency known as the Men in Black, supposedly carries out secret operations here on Earth in order to keep us safe from aliens throughout the galaxies. Here is one of their stories that "never happened"—from one of their files that "doesn't exist."

An unconvincing STARFIELD. PETER GRAVES narrates…

PETER GRAVES (v.o.) Nineteen seventy-eight. The devastating War of Zartha had raged on for fifty years.

We see a low-budget re-creation of this epic event. A bad flying saucer goes by.

JAY Hmm. Looks like Spielberg's work.

Jay sits next to Kay. The tape continues.

PETER GRAVES (v.o.) But the Zarthans had a great treasure. The Light of Zartha. A source of power so awesome, it alone could mean victory and restoration for the Zarthans…or complete annihilation if it

fell into the hands of the Kylothians. A decision was made to hide it on an insignificant blue planet, third from the Sun. A group of Zarthans made the journey led by the Keeper of the Light…
KAY Lauranna.
PETER GRAVES (v.o.) …Princess Lauranna.

Jay and Newton look at Kay, who is now totally transfixed.

PETER GRAVES (v.o.) Lauranna beseeched the Men in Black to help her hide the light on Earth. But they could not intervene…

We see actors playing MIB Agents, Kylothians, and Zarthans—standing in a cornfield.

KAY No. It was night.

EXT. MIDWEST FIELD—NIGHT—ACTUAL EVENT—25 YEARS EARLIER

A FLASH OF LIGHTNING

KAY (o.c.) It was raining.

A RAINSTORM. Kay and other AGENTS are gathered in the field.

A HOODED MASS OF NEURAL ROOTS approaches Kay.

SERLEENA You've been very wise.

We hear a WOMAN'S VOICE.

WOMAN (o.c.) Kay. Please.

Kay turns to the beautiful PRINCESS LAURANNA. Raindrops run down her face like tears.

AMBASSADOR LAURANNA If Serleena takes the Light, it is the end of our world.
KAY Madame Ambassador, if we extend protection for the Light beyond Earth, we put the Earth itself in jeopardy. We have no choice. We must remain neutral.
SERLEENA Where is it?
KAY We're neutral. Remember? If you want it…

Kay hits a button on his watch.

A SPACESHIP BLASTS OUT OF A SILO and rockets toward the heavens.

KAY Go get it.
SERLEENA NO!!

Serleena runs to her spacecraft. She turns and raises her weapon from inside her ship…

…and FIRES. Lauranna falls. MIB AGENTS fire on the ship as it takes off in the background.

Kay reaches down to Lauranna. He opens his hand. He's holding A BRACELET.

INT. NEWTON'S ROOM—NIGHT

KAY—pain in his eyes. Graves continues in the background.

PETER GRAVES (o.c.) ...And so, never knowing it happened, the people of Earth were once again saved by a secret society of protectors...

Kay stops the tape.

KAY I shouldn't have...
JAY You never sent it off the planet. You hid it here.
KAY The worm guys.

Kay runs out.

NEWTON'S MOM (o.c.) *(to Kay)* Are you one of Newton's friends from group therapy?
KAY (o.c.) Yes, ma'am. I am.
(re: the neuralyzer)
Would you look here, please.
NEWTON'S MOM (o.c.) Would you like some mini-pizzas?
Jay holds up his neuralyzer in front of Hailey and Newton.
NEWTON *(in awe)* A neuralyzer.

FLASH.

JAY Okay, first...Get some contact lenses, 'cause those joints look like they can pick up cable. Second, take her to Cambodia, get her a lobster dinner, pay more than a dollar. Third, the second you get back from Cambodia, move your bum ass out of your mom's house!
KAY (o.s.) Let's go, bud.
JAY Boy, you're like 40 years old!
KAY (o.s.) Agent Jay.
JAY All right, all right.
(to Newton and Hailey)
Oh, and there ain't no such thing as aliens or Men in Black.

Jay exits. Newton takes his glasses off and turns to Hailey.

NEWTON You want to go to Cambodia?
HAILEY Yeah.

Newton gets up from the couch, picks up a shovel.

NEWTON Hey, Mom...?

They exit.

INT./EXT. MERCEDES-BENZ

JAY Communicator. Jay.

LAURA (o.s.) Hello?
JAY Laura, it's me.

INT. WORM GUYS' APARTMENT—KITCHEN—NIGHT

Laura speaks into Jay's communicator.

LAURA Jay. We're playing Twister.

The WORMS are in various contorted positions playing TWISTER. Laura is also in a contorted position in the middle of them.

WORMS Hey, what's up, Jay? Quit touchin' my butt. Sorry, I thought it was your face.
LAURA They're pretty good at this. They don't have any spines. Oh, they were telling me about Oprah. From Chicago?
WORMS *(laughing)* Maybe *landed* in Chicago!

INT./EXT. MERCEDES-BENZ—NIGHT

Jay and Kay are there. Cut back and forth.

JAY Are you wearing a bracelet?

Laura looks at her charm bracelet.

LAURA Yeah.
KAY Is it glowing?

A LITTLE PYRAMID IS GLOWING.

LAURA It's never done that before.
JAY We're on our way.

Click.

The Mercedes-Benz takes off.

Jay hits a button on his car communicator. Click on the other end.

JAY Communicator. Frank.

INT. MIB HEADQUARTERS—MAIN ROOM—CONTINUOUS

CLOSE—FRANK'S COMMUNICATOR

JAY (o.c.) *(on the communicator)* Frank, get down to Sub Control Level C. Deactivate the lock down. We're on our way to the worm guys. We found the Light.

TILT UP TO: SERLEENA

Holding Frank's communicator. Frank is bound and gagged behind her.

SERLEENA *(imitating Frank's voice)* Got it, Jay!
(in her own voice) Scrad!

As Serleena exits...

FRANK *(mumbling, through his gag)* Bitch.

INT. MERCEDES-BENZ—NIGHT—CONTINUOUS

KAY Why didn't you say, "I love you"?
JAY He's a dog. I don't even like him.
KAY No, the girl. You're sweet on her.
JAY Hey, Kay.
KAY It's why you didn't neuralyze her. You got emotionally involved.
JAY Yeah. Like you did with Lauranna?
KAY I put the entire planet in danger because I got emotionally involved. I don't want to see you making my mistakes.

INT. WORM GUYS' APARTMENT—NIGHT—SHORT TIME LATER

The door is kicked in. Jay and Kay enter. Inside is the smoldering remains of a war zone.

JAY Laura!

Jay joins Kay to see a horrible sight.

JAY Damn!

THE WORM GUYS are on the ground CUT INTO TWO PIECES.

JAY There's still half a chance.

We hear a MOAN. One of the worms, NEEBLE opens his eyes and looks around. He sees his body is cut in half.

NEEBLE Ho boy.

Suddenly a pair of eyes on his lower half spring open. It has become a separate worm.

UPPER NEEBLE That's gonna leave a scar.
LOWER NEEBLE Who needs a martini?
UPPER NEEBLE Count me in.
JAY Where's Laura?
NEEBLE MIB headquarters. Some dumb two-headed guy.
KAY They got the bracelet...We've got thirty-nine minutes. You guys pull yourselves together.

Kay exits.

JAY Damn!

Jay exits. Off worms growing back together...

NEEBLE Oh, that's feeling better. Hey, guys. Hold on. Let me grab my drink.

INT. APARTMENT—NIGHT—SHORT TIME LATER

A FAMILY OF THREE is sitting on a sofa, watching Martha Stewart on TV. THE DOOR IS KICKED IN. Kay enters.

KAY Don't worry about a thing, folks. I used to live here. Came by to pick up a few things.

They stare in stunned silence as Kay goes to a wall, opens a panel and flips a switch. THE ENTIRE WALL FLIPS, revealing A HUGE ROOM FILLED WITH LETHAL MIB WEAPONS.

Kay grabs the weapons—and tosses them out to Jay and the Worm Guys as they enter.

WORM GUYS Wow, one fission carbonizer, one neutron destabilizer. Lookin' for a few good worms.

Kay flips the wall back and crosses out of the apartment with a duffle bag filled with weapons. The Worm Guys follow.

Jay walks up to the catatonic couple.

NEURALYZER FLASH.

KAY You did not see a room full of shiny weapons, you did not see four alien nightcrawlers. You will cherish and love each other for the rest of your lives...
JAY Which could be the next 27 or 28 minutes, so you all should get to loving and cherishing.

INT. ROOF LAUNCH PAD—CONTINUOUS

CAMERA TRACKS OVERHEAD. A DOZEN ALIEN SPACESHIPS have been dismantled and stripped of parts. We settle on JARRA and the INCREDIBLE SHIP he has fabricated for Serleena's escape.

He turns to a camera and sees Serleena on an EGG SCREEN.

ON EGG SCREEN—SERLEENA'S POV

JARRA The ship is ready.

INT. ZED'S OFFICE—CONTINUOUS

Scrad/Charlie is there with Serleena. She sees Jarra on the Egg Screen.

SERLEENA I'm on my way.

She hands Scrad/Charlie A ROUND METAL ORB.

SERLEENA Proton imploder and its detonator. Powerful enough to destroy MIB headquarters. Once I'm gone, use it.
SCRAD/CHARLIE Yes, ma'am.

EXT. MIB HEADQUARTERS—NIGHT—MOMENTS LATER

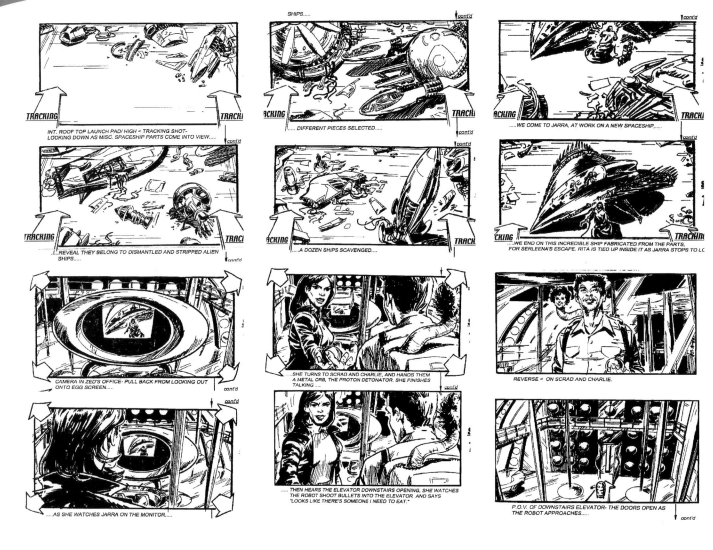

INT. ROOF TOP LAUNCH PAD/ HIGH < TRACKING SHOT- LOOKING DOWN AS MISC. SPACESHIP PARTS COME INTO VIEW......

SHIPS.....
..... DIFFERENT PIECES SELECTED.....

.....WE COME TO JARRA, AT WORK ON A NEW SPACESHIP,.....

....REVEAL THEY BELONG TO DISMANTLED AND STRIPPED ALIEN SHIPS.....

.....A DOZEN SHIPS SCAVENGED....

.....WE END ON THIS INCREDIBLE SHIP FABRICATED FROM THE PARTS, FOR SERLEENA'S ESCAPE. RITA IS TIED UP INSIDE IT AS JARRA STOPS TO LC

CAMERA IN ZED'S OFFICE- PULL BACK FROM LOOKING OUT ONTO EGG SCREEN.....

.....SHE TURNS TO SCRAD AND CHARLIE, AND HANDS THEM A METAL ORB, THE PROTON DETONATOR. SHE FINISHES TALKING....

REVERSE < ON SCRAD AND CHARLIE.

.....AS SHE WATCHES JARRA ON THE MONITOR.....

..... THEN HEARS THE ELEVATOR DOWNSTAIRS OPENING, SHE WATCHES THE ROBOT SHOOT BULLETS INTO THE ELEVATOR AND SAYS "LOOKS LIKE THERE'S SOMEONE I NEED TO EAT."

P.O.V. OF DOWNSTAIRS ELEVATOR- THE DOORS OPEN AS THE ROBOT APPROACHES.....

Jay and Kay pull their weapons from the trunk of the Mercedes.

Kay looks over his shoulder.

KAY *(to the Worm Guys)* Ready, guys?

THE WORM GUYS are strapping on bandoliers and knives. They are also wearing camouflage makeup. WE DOLLY into their serious worm faces.

NEEBLE Lock and load, baby.
KAY You ready, kid?
JAY Kid? You know, while you were away licking stamps, I saved the world from a Kreelon invasion.
KAY Kreelons are the Back Street Boys of the universe. What did they do, throw snowballs at you?

Jay raises his BAZOOKA.

KAY Do you know what you're doing?
JAY Yep. I'm about to attack one of the most feared aliens in the universe with four worms and a mailman. Let's make it hot.
KAY No, wait!

BOOM! The front door is blown away.

JAY For what?

WHOOSH...Jay, Kay, and the Worms are literally SUCKED OFF THEIR FEET INTO MIB.

INT. MIB ENTRANCE—CONTINUOUS

Jay, Kay, and the Worms burst in. Leaves, papers, and a Sabretts hot dog cart are sucked in behind them. Jay, Kay, and the Worms land in front of the GUARD AND THE HUGE FAN.

KAY Code 101 lock down.
JAY I know, I know. The building is pressurized and nothing in, nothing out. I knew that!
KAY Yeah, you knew that! Front and center, worms!

They look at the GUARD, who is chained to his seat. He continues to read his paper.

GUARD 'Bout time you guys got here. That pretty lady in there is causing all kinds of hell.

INT. MAIN HALL—CONTINUOUS

DING. The elevator doors open. The inside is RIDDLED WITH HUNDREDS OF ROUNDS OF BULLETS, being fired by THE LITTLE ALIEN ROBOT. The elevator is empty.

CAMERA BOOMS to reveal Jay, Kay, and The Worms splayed across the ceiling as the bullets continue to pump in under them.

INT. ZED'S OFFICE—CONTINUOUS

Serleena looks down to see the shooting.

As she exits.

SERLEENA Oh, yummy. Someone I need to eat.

INT. ELEVATOR—AT THE SAME TIME

Jay, Kay, and the Worms splayed on the ceiling.

KAY *(to Jay)* Get to the launch pad on the roof. The bracelet shows the departure point. No matter what happens, do not come back for me. That's an order.
JAY What do you mean?
KAY Do not come back for me.

Jay nods.

JAY Worm Guys. Give me some cover fire.

They look at the Worms, who are trembling with fear.

SLEEBLE Too scared. Can't move.

Kay turns to Jay. He shakes his head in disbelief.

With his feet pressed to either side of the elevator, Kay swings down. Upside down and weapons in each hand, he blasts away at THE LITTLE ALIEN ROBOT, driving it back.

Jay drops down and makes a break for the elevator to the roof, shoot-

ing as he goes. He gets on. The doors close.

Kay does an inverted stomach crunch, taking him up out of the line of fire of the ROBOT.

GEEBLE Limber.
KAY Get to Sub Control Panel 7 R Delta. Shut off all the power to MIB. They won't be able to launch.
SLEEBLE Too scared.

Kay opens a hatch on the ceiling of the elevator.

GEEBLE Oh, that way.
SLEEBLE Away from the bullets.
GEEBLE No problem. Ho-aw.

The Worms go.

Kay hears the LITTLE ROBOT whirring toward the elevator.

He takes out a grenade—hits the BASEMENT BUTTON—and as the ROBOT enters the elevator—he swings out over the top of the ROBOT, tossing the grenade back over his shoulder. The elevator doors close. A long beat. BOOM. Smoke.

Kay turns and runs directly into NEURAL ROOTS, which wrap around his throat.

SERLEENA Nice to see you again, Kay.

EXT. MIB ROOF—CONTINUOUS

Jay exits the elevator. The ship is powering up, ready to go.

LAURA (o.s.) Jay!
COMPUTER VOICE Three minutes to launch.

JARRA FLOATS out between Jay and the spaceship.

JARRA Hello, Jay, long time.
JAY Jarra. What's up, man. Wow, you look great. What's it been? Five years?

As Jarra floats toward him...

JARRA ...and 42 days thanks to you. You count every one when you're locked away like a primate.
JAY You shouldn't have been trying to steal our ozone.
(looks over Jarra's shoulder)
Be there in one minute, sweetie.

Jarra's capes drop. The bottom half of his torso is a PERSONAL FLYING SAUCER. SIX SMALLER, BUT IDENTICAL JARRA/SAUCER MEN FLY OUT. METAL TENTACLES hang from their spacecraft bottoms. Jay does a quick inventory.

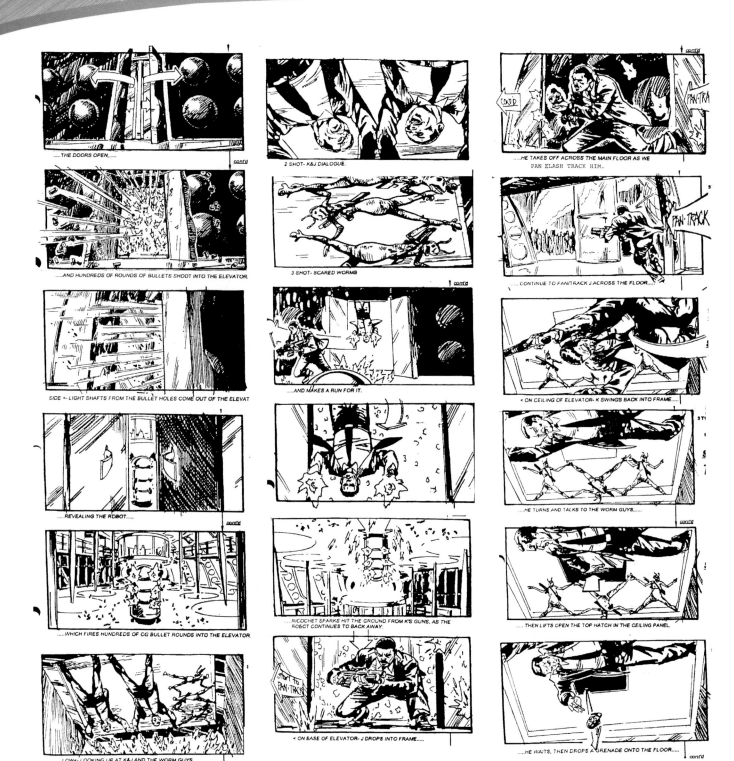

.....THE DOORS OPEN,.....

2 SHOT- K&J DIALOGUE.

.....HE TAKES OFF ACROSS THE MAIN FLOOR AS WE PAN/FLASH TRACK HIM.

.....AND HUNDREDS OF ROUNDS OF BULLETS SHOOT INTO THE ELEVATOR.

3 SHOT- SCARED WORMS

..... CONTINUE TO PAN/TRACK J ACROSS THE FLOOR.....

SIDE ← LIGHT SHAFTS FROM THE BULLET HOLES COME OUT OF THE ELEVAT

.....AND MAKES A RUN FOR IT.

< ON CEILING OF ELEVATOR- K SWINGS BACK INTO FRAME.....

.....REVEALING THE ROBOT.....

.....HE TURNS AND TALKS TO THE WORM GUYS,.....

.....WHICH FIRES HUNDREDS OF CG BULLET ROUNDS INTO THE ELEVATOR.

.....RICOCHET SPARKS HIT THE GROUND FROM K'S GUNS, AS THE ROBOT CONTINUES TO BACK AWAY.

..... THEN LIFTS OPEN THE TOP HATCH IN THE CEILING PANEL.

LOW← LOOKING UP AT K&J AND THE WORM GUYS STRETCHED OUT ON THE CEILING OF THE ELEVATOR......

< ON BASE OF ELEVATOR- J DROPS INTO FRAME.....

.....HE WAITS, THEN DROPS A GRENADE ONTO THE FLOOR.....

JAY I need to take the girl with me.
JARRA Over our dead titanium bodies.
JAY Two minutes.

JARRA'S TENTACLE WHACKS Jay in the face, sending him reeling.

JAY Oh, let's play this one by ear.

INT. MIB VENT SHAFT—AT THE SAME TIME

The armed Worm Guys make their way to the control panel.

WORMS Wrecked him? Damn near killed him.

They laugh.

WORMS So considering how late it is, this is definitely double-time, right? Plus danger pay.

INT. MAIN HALL—CONTINUOUS

Kay is thrown into a wall, knocking the wind out of him.

Neural roots pulse under the skin of Serleena's face.

KAY I should've vaporized you when I had the chance.

SERLEENA You really did love Lauranna, didn't you, Kay? You silly little man.

Serleena licks his ear.

INT. ROOF—AT THE SAME TIME

Jay faces a LINE OF THE LITTLE JARRAS. They race up to him and begin KICKING HIM WITH THEIR TENTACLES from all sides. Jay picks a PIECE OF PIPE off the floor and begins swinging at them wildly. They back off, then zip in, giving him a kick. Jay manages to WHACK ONE OF THEM, who FLIPS OVER several times before going down and shattering. One down, five to go...

INT. ROOF—AT THE SAME TIME

Jay is trapped. The CIRCLE OF SPINNING JARRA SAUCERS TIGHTENS.

One of the JARRAS comes in LOW knocking Jay off his feet. Jay lands hard on his ass.

COMPUTER VOICE Two minutes to launch.
LAURA Just go! I'll be fine!
JAY What you talking about, girl? I'm with it.

He picks up a pipe.

JAY Jarra, you're under arrest and double-fined for being that ugly and making that many copies. Now surrender!

JARRA I want him in pieces.

They converge.

He bats the unconscious Jarra into the oncoming Jarras—hitting the front JARRA head on. He ricochets into the two behind him like bowling pins.

JAY Jarra junior is going, going, gone.

They spin out of control—The back two meet in midair and explode.

INT. MIB HALLWAY—CONTINUOUS

SCRAD/CHARLIE—carrying the PROTON DETONATOR — runs down a hallway.

CHARLIE We cannot set that detonator.
SCRAD We were given an order.
CHARLIE By who? Worm lady?
SCRAD Shut up.
CHARLIE I love you, but you've given me no choice.

Charlie wills Scrad's hands up in front of him. Scrad looks shocked. His own hands grab Scrad's face and FLIP HIM OVER. They do a MIDAIR CARTWHEEL and end up standing.

SCRAD You no good son of a...

EXT. ROOF

Jay has jumped onto Jarra.

JAY You are going to die a horrible death.
(to Laura)
Laura, I'm fine, I'll be there in just a minute.
JARRA No, he won't.
JAY Was I talking to you?
JARRA Maybe I was talking to you.
JAY Well, maybe I wasn't listening.
JARRA How'd you know I was talking?
COMPUTER VOICE One minute to launch, one minute to launch.

Another Jarra approaches. Jay punches him in the face. He explodes.

JAY Down to one now, Jarra. What you gonna do, boy?

Jay detaches himself from Jarra and falls into a pile on the floor. As he tries to get up we hear:

COMPUTER VOICE Thirty seconds to launch.
(beat)
Fifteen seconds to launch.
(then)

Ten seconds to launch.
(then)
Eight, seven, six, five, four, three, two...

Jay runs to the control panel on the ship.

He hits some switches.

COMPUTER VOICE Launch terminated.
JAY What do you mean just leave you. I never run out on a fight.
LAURA Well, he took your gun, cracked you on the head...
JAY ...and?
LAURA Slammed you across the room. Half the time you were on your back.
JAY Look, that's how I fight.

INT. MAIN HALL—CONTINUOUS

Kay is being choked within a breath of his life. Serleena loosens her grip.

SERLEENA Have to run, Kay.

Sharp neural roots extend from her fingers. She grabs Kay in the middle of his chest and begins pulling as other roots wrap around him.

SERLEENA Golly, just think of the carnage and destruction that's about to happen all because you went mushy.
KAY I'll give you one last chance to surrender, you slimy Kylothian invertebrate.
SERLEENA What're you going to do to stop me?
KAY Not me. Him.

Kay looks over Serleena's shoulder to Jay, holding the antique over-under shotgun.

JAY Your flight's been canceled.

Jay BLOWS SERLEENA TO SMITHEREENS.

INT. MIB SUB-CONTROL ROOM—NIGHT

Mannix slides down a shoot and drops into a chair at the control console. The other Worms peek over the shoot.

He lowers himself to the computer keyboard. Types...

MANNIX Shut down power. Shut down power. Buttons, buttons. I'm guessing...yeah...

INT. MAIN HALL HEADQUARTERS—CONTINUOUS

Jay, Kay, and Laura are there. The place goes BLACK.

KAY Worms.

We hear the BEEP BEEP of Jay's key chain. The Mercedes—headlights on—pulls into the Main Room with the AUTO PILOT GUY behind the wheel.

Jay and Kay go to the driver's door. Jay flips him the keys. As he circles to the passenger's side...

JAY Give me the bracelet.
LAURA I'm going with you.
JAY Please give me the bracelet...
KAY Everybody in the car. Everybody.

Jay gives Kay a look. They get in. Kay throws it into gear.

INT. MIB HEADQUARTERS—CONTINUOUS

The car drops out of sight.

INT. ZED'S OFFICE

Dark. We hear a TINY SCRATCHING SOUND. WE PAN BACK to the SPLATTERED PIECES OF NEURAL ROOTS on the floor.

ONE SURVIVING NEURAL ROOT PULSES...

EXT. NYC STREET/ MERCEDES—CONTINUOUS

The MERCEDES shoots up out of the tunnel—hits the pavement — and screeches around a corner.

INT. MERCEDES—CONTINUOUS

LAURA I can't believe this charm bracelet is what everybody's been after.
JAY You'd be surprised how often it's something small like that.
KAY The bracelet is telling us the departure point.
JAY What?!
KAY It's also a fail-safe device. If we don't get to that departure point in 11 minutes and 15 seconds, that bracelet's going to go nuclear and destroy all life on Earth.
LAURA What?!

The Mercedes is bumped. Kay turns.

EXT. SKY—CONTINUOUS

Serleena's NEW SPACESHIP swoops into frame, BUMPING THEM AGAIN.

Kay looks at his watch, then the infamous LITTLE RED BUTTON.

JAY Kay, no!
KAY I know what I'm doing, slick.
JAY NO!

Too late. Kay's already hit the RED BUTTON.

The car accelerates down the street like a STREAK.

THE ENTIRE DASH INCLUDING THE STEERING WHEEL DISAP-PEARS. Kay turns to Jay.

JAY Modified to hyper-speed.

KAY Seat belts.

INT./EXT. MERCEDES-BENZ—CONTINUOUS

THE NAVIGATION STALK APPEARS. A high-tech version of the SONY PLAYSTATION 2 CONTROLLER. Everyone is pinned against the seats.

KAY What's that?

JAY At hyper-speed you have to use the navigational stalk.

KAY Oh, God.

Kay grabs the STALK.

THE MERCEDES-BENZ does a ROLL around a corner, sending everyone flying.

JAY IS ON TOP OF LAURA.

LAURA If we die...

JAY Kay, use the toggle switches to activate the right and left ailerons. Use the joystick for the stabilizer and rudder.

KAY Oh.

Kay hits the switches.

THE MERCEDES-BENZ FLIPS UPSIDE DOWN.

LAURA LANDS ON TOP OF JAY.

LAURA ...I just want you to know you're the only person I ever loved.

JAY You know—hold onto that thought for one second.

Serleena fires a TORPEDO. BANG! The Mercedes-Benz, covered in flames, speeds through the fireball, but starts spinning out of control.

EXT. NEW YORK STREET/ MERCEDES-BENZ—CONTINUOUS

Out of control.

JAY/KAY/LAURA Ahhhh!!!

INT. MERCEDES-BENZ—CONTINUOUS

Jay inches his way to the front seat—straining against the G-force.

JAY *(to Laura)* Communicator! Worms!!

INT. MAIN HALL—CONTINUOUS

The WORMS are there, SMOKING CIGARS. Frank is getting a light.

FRANK So I said, listen, bitch, if you don't want me to kick your skinny Zone Diet ass, turn around and exit the planet.
JAY (o.c.) *(on speaker)* WORMS!! Where are you?
FRANK Main Hall. Egg display.

INT. MAIN HALL—CONTINUOUS

We hear Jay over communicator speaker.

JAY (o.c.) Okay, lost control...We're taking fire. Kay pushed the red button. Computer at MIB can lock on and destroy bogey. I'll walk you through it...

Sleeble turns to the EGG SCREEN.

A ROW OF BARS BLINKS ALONG THE BOTTOM. "COMPUTER SHUT DOWN IMPROPERLY. RE-CONFIGURING HARD DRIVE. SEVEN MINUTES REMAINING."

SLEEBLE Uhh, Jay...when we turned off the electricity, we may have forgotten to shut it down exactly properly...

They hear A TORPEDO BLAST over the speakers.

Frank pushes his way to the microphone.

FRANK *(grave)* Jay? Frank. You were the best darn partner a Remoolian could ever have. Godspeed.

Frank hangs up.

JAY Frank! Frank!

INT./EXT MERCEDES-BENZ—CONTINUOUS

Jay can't believe he hung up.

Kay looks down at the STALK.

KAY Okay, here we go.
(hits button)
Automatic pilot...

The INFLATABLE AUTO-PILOT sits on KAY'S LAP.

His hands dangle uselessly at his sides.

KAY It's not automatic piloting.
JAY He doesn't operate at hyper-speed.
KAY I could really use a steering wheel here!
JAY We don't have no damn steering wheel. This is what we got.

Kay tries to reach around him, pushing AUTO-PILOT on the stalk.

They CORKSCREW wildly like a Fourth of July firework.

Jay appears from under the dash and tries to fight his way to the controls as he's tossed around the interior of the car...

JAY Didn't your mother ever give you a Game Boy?
KAY What is a Game Boy?
JAY Move!

Kay and Jay struggle to switch seats.

JAY Hey, that's not the navigational stalk.

They finally do. Jay grabs the controls.

Jay expertly rights the Mercedes-Benz and BARREL-ROLLS away. Serleena loses ground, but follows.

EXT. SERLEENA'S SHIP—CONTINUOUS

Her ship bears down on the Mercedes-Benz. She has them directly in her sights and fires.

EXT. NEW YORK STREET/ MERCEDES-BENZ—CONTINUOUS

Jay sees the TORPEDO behind him.

At the last possible instant, he gives the controls a tiny flick of the wrist. The MERCEDES-BENZ makes A HARD RIGHT. Serleena's torpedo explodes just beyond them.

Jay looks below. He spots something.

JAY Okay. Straight down!

He slams the stick forward.

The MERCEDES-BENZ heads STRAIGHT DOWN.

LAURA No! Down is bad.

It looks like they're headed directly for the pavement.

LAURA Straight down is idiotic!

Jay pulls back lightly on the stick.

EXT. SUBWAY ENTRANCE—CONTINUOUS

The MERCEDES-BENZ flies down into the entrance. Not an inch to spare. After a beat, Serleena follows. SWOOSH...

INT. SUBWAY TUNNEL—CONTINUOUS

The MERCEDES-BENZ banks into the TUNNEL and disappears.

SERLEENA tries to keep pace, taking out a chunk of wall that reads: CHAMBERS ST. STATION...and heads down the same tunnel.

No one even looks up from their papers.

INT. SUBWAY TUNNEL/MERCEDES-BENZ/SERLEENA'S SPACECRAFT

HIGH-POWERED HALOGEN HEADLIGHTS illuminate the track ahead.

SERLEENA Idiots.

She gives them a hard bump. The Mercedes-Benz goes sideways, taking out a chunk of concrete and rebar wall.

Serleena retreats, taking a look at the damage.

The MERCEDES-BENZ'S BACK END IS SMASHED IN.

Serleena BUMPS them again. Sparks fly from electrical wiring.

KAY Subway may not be the best place to lose her.
JAY Where is he?
KAY He?

Kay and Laura make out A SHAPE ahead of them.

JAY Jeff.
KAY Jeff?
LAURA Jeff?

SCREECH!!! Jeff sees Jay in the front seat of the car. Jay waves. SCREECH!!! As they get closer, JEFF OPENS HIS GIANT JAWS.

JAY/KAY/LAURA Jeff!

SERLEENA is right on top of them.

Jay SHUTS DOWN THE THROTTLE.

They STOP. INSTANTLY. The MERCEDES-BENZ DROPS like a stone on the subway tracks. The automatic pilot inflates.

EXT. ROOFTOP—MOMENTS LATER

A ROOFTOP. The Statue of Liberty is in the distance. Other rooftops around us. The Mercedes-Benz roars in and screeches to a stop. Jay, Kay, and Laura get out.

JAY Runnin' out of time, Kay. Where is the Light?

Kay questions Laura.

KAY A code...Think, Laura. A combination...Anything. Did Ben ever say anything to you about a code? A special date? Anything?

Laura struggles with his line of questioning, but racks her memory. Everyone exchanges looks.

LAURA There was a...song Ben used to sing to me when I was little. A lullaby..."4, 3, 2, I love you; 7, 8, 9, ain't that fine..." I still sing it when I can't sleep. But that can't be...

Kay cuts her off and grabs the bracelet, dialing in the numbers.

KAY It's the code. It will activate the light.

Jay takes the PIZZA PARLOR NAPKIN out of his pocket. He holds it up. The LOGO ALIGNS PERFECTLY with where they are standing. GLASS PYRAMID. STATUE OF LIBERTY IN THE DISTANCE. A STAR ABOVE IT.

As Kay finishes punching in the number, Jay looks up at the star above Miss Liberty. A beam shoots out of the star, turning a large decorative rock on their rooftop into a space capsule.

At the same time, A HIDEOUS SOUND. JEFF comes crashing up through the GLASS PYRAMID. ROARRR.....

JAY Jeff! I am so not in the mood for you. Get back in the subway right now.

RIPPP...Jeff's skin peels back revealing a NIGHTMARISH NEURAL-ROOTED SERLEENA CREATURE inside. Genetically disturbing.

KAY That's not good.

Kay grabs Laura and pulls her away.

Serleena spots Laura and the bracelet. A NEURAL ROOT lashes out to grab her. Jay shoves Laura out of harm's way...into Kay's arms. The root wraps around Jay's throat, yanking him back instead.

JAY Ahhhh....

Jay is PULLED TOWARD SERLEENA, who starts whipping roots around his body, engulfing him.

SERLEENA/CREATURE sees Kay and Laura running. She leans forward toward them.

Laura stops and stares in disbelief.

LAURA Jay!
JAY Kay! A little help!

Kay FIRES his weapon, knocking Serleena back.

KAY Laura! Get the bracelet on the pod!

BANG! He fires again.

Jay's HEAD pops out of the gaping HOLE.

He's sucked back in.

He FIRES again. Serleena makes a move toward Kay and Laura. Kay FIRES again.

Jay's SHOULDER pops out of Serleena's neural-rooted body. It's smoking.

JAY (o.c.) *(from inside)* Aim higher!
KAY He's fine.

Kay fires at Serleena's face. POW! It distorts it and knocks her down...but she staggers forward toward Kay and Laura.

KAY He does this all the time.

BANG! Laura looks at him. He FIRES again.

KAY Laura! The bracelet!

Laura moves to the transporter, placing the bracelet inside.

Jay's head pops out, upside down.

JAY You're just making her mad, Kay.

BANG!—Kay fires. Jay is yanked back in.

Jay's head pops out from another spot.

JAY We need...

BANG! BANG!—Kay fires. Jay pops out from a third spot.

JAY ...a bigger—

BANG! BANG! BANG! Kay fires.

JAY —WEAPON!

BANG! BANG! BANG! BANG! BANG!

ANGLE ON: SCRAD

Holding the bomb Serleena gave them.

SCRAD Proton bomb?

Jay's head pops out of her mouth.

JAY Thank you!

Jay's hands reach out of her mouth. Scrad throws the proton bomb to him.

JAY Where's the detonator?!
CHARLIE We broke it.

JAY Kay, shoot them! Shoot them!

BLAM! BLAM! BLAM! BLAM! BLAM! from Kay. Jay does a back flip out of Serleena's mouth and slam-dunks the proton bomb down her throat.

EXT. SERLEENA—CONTINUOUS

Jay lands on the rooftop. The CREATURE looks toward the CAPSULE, which heads toward the STAR BEAM.

Serleena takes off at a GALLOP, starting to grow wings and fly.

Jay and Kay run to their Mercedes to get their big weapons from its trunk.

Jay nods to Kay. They slam down the actions on their weapons. They raise their weapons to their shoulders and follow Serleena's path with raised guns.

KAY Kid?
JAY Yeah?
KAY Thanks for bringing me back.
JAY No problem.

He sneaks a look at Laura, standing stunned near the car. Kay notices.

They track Serleena galloping toward the transport Sphere as if on a clay target range. BANG. BANG.

The two shots hit Serleena just as her neural roots begin to wrap around the Sphere.

Serleena looks to the two smoking wounds, then to Jay and Kay, who give her a little wave.

Serleena EXPLODES IN A BEAUTIFUL DISPLAY OF FIREWORKS.

The SPHERE DISAPPEARS in a CRACKLING ENERGY BURST. Everyone shields their eyes. Then it's quiet.

Jay and Kay look out as the fireworks dissipate, leaving an ethereal glow over New York. As they watch:

JAY So what's it like on the outside? Not doing this every day?
KAY It was...nice. Sleep late on weekends, watch the Weather

Channel...

His eyes gaze across the skyline as Jay gazes at Laura.

KAY *(turning to Jay)* I went offbook twenty-five years ago and it almost destroyed the planet.

He looks at Laura and back to Jay.

KAY It's your decision. You'll do the right thing.

Realizing that "we are who we are," Jay walks over to Laura, pulling out his neuralyzer, preparing to finally flash her.

JAY I just want you to know you're the only person I've ever loved.

FLASH.

JAY The City of New York would like to thank you for participating in our...architectural survey.

As Laura is led away by MIB personnel.

JAY Maybe we can have some pie sometime.
SCRAD/CHARLIE Hey, what about us?
KAY There's always an opening at the post office.
SCRAD/CHARLIE Post office? Yes!!

Jay and Kay take a long look at each other.

KAY Come on. Let's get going.

Jay and Kay turn and walk—the Statue of Liberty in the background.

JAY Get going? Thousands of people in New York and Jersey just saw our little event. Plan needs to be thought out. A plan needs to be cool.

Kay lifts up his PULSAR watch and pushes a button.

KAY Kid...I'll get you trained yet.

WE BOOM UP AS behind them the TORCH ON THE STATUE OF LIBERTY lights up. A HUGE NEURALYZER FLASH.

KAY You didn't really think I put Earth in jeopardy without a back-up plan, did you, slick?
JAY I want one of those.

THE END

Columbia Pictures Presents
An Amblin Entertainment Production

In Association with MacDonald/Parkes Productions
A Barry Sonnenfeld Film

Director - Barry Sonnenfeld
Screenplay by Robert Gordon and Barry Fanaro
Story by Robert Gordon
Based on the Malibu Comic by Lowell Cunningham
Producers - Walter F. Parkes and Laurie MacDonald
Executive Producer - Steven Spielberg
Co-Producer - Graham Place
Director of Photography - Greg Gardiner
Production Designer - Bo Welch
Editors - Steven Weisberg and Richard Pearson
Music by Danny Elfman
Alien Make-Up Effects by Rick Baker
Special Animation and Visual Effects by Industrial Light & Magic
Costume Designer - Mary E. Vogt
Tommy Lee Jones as Agent Kay
Will Smith as Agent Jay
Lara Flynn Boyle as Serleena
Johnny Knoxville as Scrad/Charlie
Rosario Dawson as Laura
Tony Shalhoub as Jeebs
Rip Torn as Zed

ABOUT THE AUTHOR

Brad Munson has been a writer of nonfiction, fiction, and screenplays for more than twenty years. He has written regularly for *Cinefex*, the respected journal of special effects, since its earliest days, including articles on *Star Trek: The Motion Picture*, *Return to Oz*, and *Evolution*; other short nonfiction has appeared in such varied publications as *The Santa Barbara Times, Oui,* and *Firsts: Collecting Modern First Editions.* His first novel, *The Mad Throne*, was published in 1978; he has edited and ghost-written many books since then, including a series of "haunted house" sequels that shall remain nameless. His movies include *Dirty Laundry, Sunset Strip*, and a number of behind-the-scenes "script doctor" projects. A teacher, trainer, editor, and marketing consultant as well, Brad has worked in radio, comics, and book and magazine publishing, and published newsletters on everything from role-playing games to dental marketing. He lives in a charming but decrepit Craftsman home in Pasadena, California, with his wife and three daughters.